Scar

Sara Mesa

SCAR

Translated from the Spanish by Adriana Nodal-Tarafa

DALKEY ARCHIVE PRESS

Originally published in Spanish by Editorial Anagrama as *Cicatriz* in 2015.

Copyright © 2015 by Sara Mesa
Translation copyright © 2017 by Adriana Nodal-Tarafa
First Dalkey Archive edition, 2017.

Library of Congress Cataloging-in-Publication Data
Names: Mesa, Sara, 1976- author. | Nodal-Tarafa, Adriana, translator.Title:
Scar / by Sara Mesa ; translation by Adriana Nodal-Tarafa.
Other titles: Cicatriz. English
Description: First Dalkey Archive edition. | Victoria, TX : Dalkey Archive
Press, 2017.
Identifiers: LCCN 2017006155 | ISBN 9781943150274 (pbk. : alk. paper)
Subjects: LCSH: Man-woman relationships--Fiction. | Obsessive-
compulsive disorder--Fiction. | GSAFD: Romantic suspense fiction.
Classification: LCC PQ6713.E823 C5313 2017 | DDC 863/.7--dc23
LC record available at https://lccn.loc.gov/2017006155

www.dalkeyarchive.com
Victoria, TX / McLean, IL / Dublin

This work has been published with a subsidy from the Ministry of Education,
Culture and Sport of Spain.

Dalkey Archive Press publications are, in part, made possible through the
support of the University of Houston-Victoria and its programs in creative
writing, publishing, and translation.

Printed on permanent/durable acid-free paper

The car is extremely fast

and the scars are made of guilt, and guilt is, really,

a flavorless way of engaging the world.

MARTA SANZ,
Amour Fou

TRANSLATOR'S PREFACE

I
Acknowledgments

Although the bulk of a literary translator's work is performed in solitude, the translation that follows this preface is without a doubt the result of collaboration.

I was only able to contemplate rendering this specific novel by Sara Mesa in English in the first place thanks to the helpful correspondence of Paula Canal at Anagrama Press in Spain. She was immediately responsive, presenting me with options for translation that might suit the aesthetic of Dalkey Archive Press.

Just as importantly, the task assigned to me by my mentor at Dalkey Archive Press, John O'Brien, was to choose a work to translate that I found remarkably compelling: nothing short of that would do. His uncompromising insistence on passion as a central aspect of the work cemented my understanding of literary translation as an art form in itself, one that should be delved into soul first.

Scar (*Cicatriz*) did indeed enthrall me. My first reading began an afternoon in a coffee shop in Dublin, where I was attending the seminar portion of Dalkey's Applied Literary Translation program for budding literary translators. The shop eventually had to close for the evening, so I paused my reading to walk to Trinity College and resume it in my room. There were no long pauses after that. I finished reading *Scar* late that night and knew it was the book I wanted to translate. The story echoed dynamics I could personally relate to at that moment— which seemed like a strange or magical twist in the plot of my life at the time. However, I also recognized it as a unique and unsettling depiction of tensions that an entire generation currently faces, as larger systemic forces shape individual lives. The tensions Sara Mesa illustrates are present at the very least in the Global North, yet likely in urbanized areas of the Global South as well, judging by how well *Scar* has been received in Latin America. It was very obviously my kind of story, personal and collective, with more questions than answers, innovative in style, unapologetically dark.

Finally, this translation wouldn't have existed without Sara Mesa, who answered my questions, asked her own, gave me her blessing for certain modifications I will discuss in the following section, and even took the time to encourage me. I am grateful to her for approaching my questions with a collaborative spirit and for writing this story.

II

Notes about the translation

The most basic, yet important, challenge I faced was to ensure that the translated text flow naturally in the opening chapter, which is intentionally disorienting in the Spanish original. It was crucial to the story that it retain this confusing quality, but there was a risk that it could sound like an awkward translation. A few rounds of edits and feedback by John O'Brien went into this section in the beginning of the translation process.

Because the story takes place in present-day Spain, I retained the decimal system and the Euro currency, except when it came to people's height and weight, as I suspected the mental calculations may take the reader out of the story. That being said, the Cárdenas of *Scar* is a fictional city.

Where the Spanish original contained racial labels whose appropriateness is contentious in the United States and which were irrelevant to the accurate depiction of the story itself, I provided acceptable alternatives with Sara Mesa's permission. This was also an ethical stance on my part. I chose not to reiterate terms with colonial racist legacies unless absolutely necessary in order to tell the story, while maintaining the integrity of the images the author evoked.

Scar

0. SCAR

THERE IT IS, he says.

He points to the tallest building on the street—an old, reddish, sixteen-story block of concrete with uneven ledges and small windows reflecting the sunlight.

They stop on the sidewalk across the street and look up at it. It seems abandoned—shattered glass, broken blinds, old For Rent signs—but they see some names for businesses that are still open: a law office, two accounting firms, two tax consultants, a language school.

Like I said, it's almost empty, he mutters.

She nods; they cross the street.

The inside is dimly lit and overheated. The color of the worn tile in the lobby has faded. There are dust motes floating in the air, making them clear their throats. A security guard is sitting behind a wood counter, carefully examining a brochure. He doesn't ask where they're going. Expressionless, he looks at them briefly, mumbles a halfhearted greeting, and turns back to the leaflet.

The couple gets into one of the elevators and the man presses the button for the top floor.

The metal carriage screeches and vibrates like an old freight elevator. She looks down at the floor and to the sides. He looks straight at her. The floor indicator isn't working, so they focus on the flickering from the fluorescent bulb on the ceiling; it occasionally turns off completely. They won't know where they are until they feel the very last rough jolt.

They arrive at an unlit hallway that smells damp. An additional flight of stairs leads to an office on the roof, which can't be accessed by elevator. The couple walks up the steps slowly; he leads the way. A window that's almost opaque from dirt allows some light into this last room, a four-by-four-meter square where no one has been in a long time.

They come face-to-face and look each other over from top to bottom.

She has on a black silk skirt, a simple green shirt, and sandals in the same color. He's wearing linen pants, a short-sleeved polo shirt, a linen jacket, and leather shoes with a slightly narrowing tip. It's very hot, they're both sweating. They smile politely at each other, dazed by the heat.

He hands her a bag.

She takes it, puts her hand inside, and pulls out a printed blue-and-gray shirt. She hesitates, turning it over in her hands. She quickly takes off her shirt and puts on the one he just gave her. It takes her only a few seconds, enough for him to scan her back and the elegant black-lace bra.

He moves his hand slightly toward her body without touching her.

What do you think? she asks.

Good. It looks very good on you.

They smile again. He comes closer and kisses her.

She lets him. Her arms fall inertly to her sides and her back arches slightly. He then grabs her by the waist, but she remains motionless, not reciprocating.

He lets her go.

Will you be leaving it on? It goes much better with that skirt than the other one.

Another time, she replies. *I'd rather wear mine.*

They're both yours now.

She bites her lip, then insists, *I'll wear it another day.*

She changes clothes again. He watches her.

His breathing becomes faster.

A shiver runs down his legs.

Are you also wearing something of mine . . . underneath?

She nods and lowers the skirt's waistband until the edge of her pearl-colored lace underwear is visible over her pubic mound.

That's enough, he says, adding, *Thank you.*

The young woman folds the shirt carefully; she lifts her skirt back into place. She puts the shirt in the bag and gives it back. They sit still and stay awkwardly silent for a few moments. The hum of traffic is so muffled there that the silence between them seems louder; it becomes denser, uncomfortable beyond repair.

When leaving the building, just before stepping on the striped crosswalk, he turns to her. *You can tell there's a mark*, he says. His eyes shine as he speaks, she notices the movement of his pupils, which grow and shrink at times. *The C-section scar*, he adds.

Yeah, I guess you can, she admits.

Both blush. *You're quite the observer*, she says in a low voice.

I don't mind the scar, he stutters. His hand moves as if he were going to take her arm, but then stops midair, as if he were suddenly frozen. *Truly, believe me. I don't mind at all.*

1. SEVEN YEARS BEFORE

Above all, my stoic view of life prevails:
whatever happens, whichever direction
the world goes in, some will be above, others below,
some will suffer injustices, others will cause them even if
they don't want to. The only thing we can do is trust that
there's a just proportion of joyful and
painful moments. Yes: I believe in predestination.
Why then am I interested in living if I will
never be the owner of my actions, and even these words that
I write now, and the relationship I have with you, were written
long ago? The load of painful moments shrinks when you
reach that conclusion, or it becomes lighter to bear.

A METAL TABLE and some file cabinets. Next to the computer, three or four rows of card indexes. A narrow room without windows, with water-stained walls and a deep scent of bleach and ammonia. A large pot with a plastic ficus tree and a piece of chewing gum that no one bothers to remove. A charitable organization's calendar from the previous year hanging from a pillar with a few dates circled in red. The ring of the phone, the whirr of the air-conditioning unit, the life outside that never, ever slips in. Even the messenger who brings the packages doesn't take off his helmet when he comes in. His stocky figure wobbles forward; he delivers the merchandise, extends the delivery note for a signature, and leaves without letting his face be seen. There's a constant whisper coming from the desks at the end of the room. Two coworkers gossip. They don't stop their chatter, not to type, not to answer the phone—one picks up the receiver, the other one continues. The chat is lethargic, mildly apathetic, as if it were an obligation or a tired ritual.

Your daughter in college then . . .

We had to remodel the kitchen anyway, the single-handle faucet . . .

Because sometimes it's more convenient to finance, they offer comprehensive insurance . . .

Mine wants to be a veterinarian . . .

. . . with Emmental cheese and battered egg; way, way better . . .

Sonia balances on her swiveling chair in front of them, yanking out the foam that bulges from the torn leather on the armrests. Her routine is perfectly laid out. Every day she tears a sheet off a little table calendar, types the data from tens of card indexes into her computer, and then entertains herself surfing the Internet, biting her nails, and carving deeper into the armrest wound. Her job—which she considers meaningless—consists of transferring the information on the old card indexes to a database. Since the categories rarely match, she has to modify, deform, or distort them; or do whatever it takes to make them correspond. In the beginning she was tormented by doubt, she felt paralyzed by the responsibility. She would ask her coworkers and wouldn't get any responses, except mute, vacant expressions or blank and maybe—she thought—slightly offended stares. One day she heard that the database would be replaced soon. By a new system, they said. A more rational, updated one. Soon? What does *soon* mean? Tomorrow? A few months, a few years? Shrugs. Slightly open, listless mouths. Silences that hide absolutely nothing. So, in addition to being tedious, her efforts were pointless. Why would they make her work like this? she asked herself. No one supervises her work, no one checks the time she clocks in and out, or the days off she grants herself. What they're doing, she thinks, is keeping her busy. Simply keeping her occupied so she doesn't bother anyone. An intern in the municipal archive can't do much more. She can understand that.

Apathy spreads like a cancer, she thinks. Like a vine, clinging with every curve. Each day she copies fewer card indexes into the database. Each day she edits the information less. Each day she kills more and more time playing online. She finds hours of distraction mainly in chat rooms and forums: dialogs, discussions, masquerade balls, stimulating entertainment that gives her a breath of fresh air and makes the room around her feel wider.

One day she browses a literary forum where she thinks the contributors seem more interesting than in the others: they talk about books, film, they exchange political opinions and jokes wrapped in the kind of sarcasm that she finds funny. She creates a profile with a male pseudonym and immediately gets a sound alert and a red icon, a private message at the bottom of the screen. *You're new, right?* someone who identifies themselves with the name <<Clarice>> asks. *Yes*, she says, *Today is my first day. Where do you live? I live in a cabin, like in walden.* Clarice laughs. *So witty. You don't want to say? How old are you? Thirty-five*, she says. *Hmm the best age for a man*, says Clarice. Yes, Sonia's having fun. Of course she's having fun. She's always liked wearing masks.

As a child in school she used to say she was a ballerina, that her dad had died in the war, that they had a grand piano, that the family car had bulletproof windows, that her mom was Russian, and that she had a parakeet that recited the Bible by heart. Liar? She was called that many times. It left her feeling uncomfortable, disgruntled. A heavy feeling of guilt would haunt her for days. She didn't mean to deceive anyone, she now thought: she only wanted to live more lives. Her curiosity was—is—too large to confine to a single identity.

Hypatia, Mr. Fish, Postmodern Venus, Ignatius J., Fra Angélico, Sweety Kitty, Knut Hamsun, Anne Oying, El-friede, Mo Xi Co. The contributors' pseudonyms belong to men, women, old, young, people who say they're from this or that city, or who claim they do this or that for a living. Sonia thinks none of it's true. There are those who are online every day, at all times, and those who rarely let themselves be seen; some are loquacious, others laconic; some are predictable, others enigmatic; some are aggressive, others submissive; some have classic taste, others are snobs. There are also many lonely ones who try to seduce others, strange personalities that become jealous and unsettled, that pressure and compete for the group's leadership.

The confused notion of adventure vanishes as soon as she turns the computer off.

This is stupid, she tells herself.

And yet, she decides to attend a dinner that some of the forum members organize in Cárdenas, about seven hundred kilometers from her city, despite the fact that she doesn't have money or time, and that she will have to come up with a lie to make it all the way there without anyone in her family censoring that whim.

She looks at herself in the mirror again. Black dress, striped panty hose, and flats; because she hates high heels, and because it would be absurd to spend the money on shoes that are only good for wearing on certain occasions. For Sonia, the concept of an *occasion* doesn't exist. Her life doesn't offer *occasions*. The way it's set up—and she isn't sure that she's chosen this arrangement—she doesn't need to have different clothes for different moments. She turns back to the mirror in the room— the cheapest accommodation she could find in the city—and gives herself a detailed inspection wearily, thinking this should be fine for a night out. An *occasion*, she tells herself. No one will notice she's had this dress for years.

She takes a long time on the way to the restaurant. She walks window-shopping and even considering the idea of buying different panty hose and changing them before she gets there. Cárdenas to her means an ear-piercing bustle. She notices how it contrasts with her city, much more provincial and predictable. Cárdenas thumps with violence, speed, and amalgamation. She's curious about the immigrants, the street vendors, the gangs of teenagers roaming the streets, the street-food stands. She's attracted to everything that's new. Her heart beats faster as she gets close to the venue. In the nearby streets, she fantasizes about the masks unveiling. Some have exchanged pictures previously but no one has seen her and she hasn't seen anyone. She thinks it's more intriguing this way. She looks around. People cross in all directions, they advance quickly, glaring at the pavement, or they kill time thumbing on their cell phones while waiting for someone. A guy smoking. Two women chatting; one is carrying a Chihuahua. A woman with an Ecuadorian accent pushes an elderly man's wheelchair. Could that man crossing in a hurry from the sidewalk right across from her be Ignatius J.? Could he be Fra Angélico? Could Mr. Fish—so friendly, so pleasant—actually be a shy, gifted kid with acne? Is The Muse as seductive and irresistible as she always insinuates? Is Wallace S. the learned gentleman versed in poetry he seems to be? Or is he just a frustrated middle-school teacher looking for an extramarital fling with some young aspiring poet? Her intuition tells her that the more enigmatic ones, the marginal ones, those who really spark her curiosity, will not make an appearance. No, those who have something to hide, the unstable ones, the ones who are ashamed of themselves, those who feel superior or inferior to the rest, they will not be there. If anything, they will stay near the door without identifying themselves, or lean against the bar making conjectures about those who go into the reserved room. A table for twenty, they had calculated that many, although only sixteen show up in the end. Sonia is the last one to come in, dazed, hesitant, tense, and slightly disappointed because everyone is much older and more conventional than she had hoped. They're boring enough for her to realize that, once again, she's wasted her time.

This is ridiculous, she thinks, but later, as the night goes on and the glasses of wine take hold, she stops thinking about it out of sheer bewilderment.

Hi, I'm Mr. Fish . . . You are? A guy of about forty, short, with watery eyes hiding behind coke-bottle glasses and hairy hands he can't keep still for one second, leans over the table, puts his arm around her, and pinches her cheek. *You're so young!* he says.

Sonia flees the sight of him as soon as she's able. All the men who have introduced themselves to her are disappointing. It was much better online, she thinks. Much more interesting and witty. The faces she sees now are surprisingly ordinary. They are what they are, there's nothing behind their expressions: eyes, noses, cheekbones, foreheads, lips that smile, tongues that click, and teeth that chew. A woman loses her contact lens in the middle of dinner. Another, the one who goes by Clarice— short, chubby, timid—leaves abruptly after receiving a phone call. A gray-haired man addresses a sixteen-year-old boy with airs of superiority, without a doubt he's the youngest among the attendees. He pours him wine over and over again; the kid gets drunk without saying a word, without smiling once.

Many get up and switch seats during dessert. Sonia sits next to The Muse, a thirty-something-year-old who compliments her dress and panty hose. She seems to be the life of the party: all the conversations that cross paths at the table pass through her, who skillfully redirects them. Sonia listens to them speak about those who aren't there. They speculate about who they are, why they didn't show. Has anyone ever seen them? The Muse deals out more information than anyone else. She puts her hypotheses forward. The others nod, question, and laugh hysterically. Fake, histrionic laughter, Sonia thinks. The Muse turns to her.

How is it that you, coming from so far . . . ?

Oh no, it's not far at all, Sonia says. She smiles and lets someone pour her another glass of wine without giving any explanation. No one else asks her anything and she drinks in silence, bored. After dinner they divide into groups to catch cabs and go to a nightclub. On the way, Sonia contemplates the city at night and a strange melancholy comes over her. She's on the wrong side of the story, she thinks, confused. Always on the wrong side, she repeats to herself. She isn't very sure what it means but the feeling keeps her company for a few minutes, until the cab stops in front of the club's entrance and someone holds the car door open for her.

The bouncer, a large man with dark skin, stuffed into a glitter-covered suit with shoulder pads, inspects all of them before they go in. His eyes fix on Sonia's shoes, he smiles to himself, then gestures with his head that she can go in. She realizes she's out of place. All the women there are much more dressed up, with makeup and high heels. Luckily, inside the venue her outfit goes unnoticed. The darkness and the lights moving across the dance floor distort everyone's appearance with their flashes. Sonia blends in, dancing with this and that person. She loses track of time. She vaguely remembers someone trying to kiss her—she may have allowed it—someone offering her cocaine—she refused—getting in another cab—a truck drove next to it washing the street—and finally getting in bed without taking off her clothes. The pounding headache, the dry lips, and the never-ending train ride home will come in the morning.

She leans her forehead on the window, watching the landscape unfold as she travels—always the same, always identical to itself. Fields and dry, yellowing grass. Soft terrain elevations. The sky with its cirrus clouds. The protruding shapes in the periphery. Poles and more poles with their wiring. Cattle in the distance, undefined—cows, sheep? Blurry horizon. Strips of fog. Everything is the same, always same, all of the time, for kilometers and kilometers, and like that, times seven hundred.

Just when she decides to delete her forum account she gets

a private message from Knut Hamsun. Concise, unexpected. She reads it several times without knowing what to reply. Sonia has never spoken to him before. She hasn't met him either. He didn't make it to the dinner, although it looks like he lives in Cárdenas and was on the list of potential attendees. He doesn't explain his proposal in the message. An exchange, he says. *You send me a picture so I can see you. In return, I'll send you any book you ask for. You can ask for several. It's no problem.*

What does Sonia know about him? Very little, really. He rarely posts on the forum threads but, when he does, she feels uncomfortable without quite knowing why. His dry, dispassionate tone? His presumption? That air of detachment he gives off? His posturing as someone who possesses codes or knowledge the rest will never have access to? He often challenges people's views but he's polite, educated. A lone-wolf type, yet always interested in analyzing others' behavior. During the dinner it was said that he was a young man who brags about shoplifting at large department stores, that he was probably dangerous, or at least not to be trusted too much. Yet the way he expresses himself—with a somewhat archaic correctness, completely out of cultural context sometimes—doesn't fit the image of an average videogame thief.

Sonia stands up, paces around in the hallway for a minute or two. None of her coworkers look up from the screen. Sonia gets the feeling they're all absorbed in similar forums, in their chats online, in shopping or bidding sites. It's very cold in the office, some haven't even taken off their coats. Sonia looks at them for a moment before going back to her desk. When the deliveryman arrives, breathing heavily through his helmet, she's replying to Knut Hamsun. *Why the interest in seeing me?* she asks. She also forwards the message to The Muse. She wants to know what she thinks of the proposal. The deliveryman waits by her side rubbing his hands together.

Very busy, huh?

Sonia apologizes and signs the delivery note for him. When she looks back at the monitor, both answers are already blinking on her screen. Knut's: *My interest is quite simple. Someone who was at the dinner told me about you. They say you're very good-looking. That's why I want to see you. For your peace of mind, I will tell you that I don't want anything more—and nothing less—than that.* The Muse's: *I wouldn't send him anything. Or reply to him. The books he's offering are most likely stolen. Better stay away from that dude.* Sonia thanks her for the advice and replies to him immediately. *OK*, she says. *I'll see what picture I can find. I guess a normal one is fine with you. About the books*, she adds, *let me think about what titles I'm interested in.*

A sad and scant family album. The photos are disorganized, pasted on with pieces of tape that have eaten away at the color. Sonia's grandmother moves her head nervously, as if wanting to ask her something. Sonia brings her a black and white picture of a very young woman who has the same milky complexion as the white hue of the grass in the photo; she's sitting cross-legged on a blanket in the countryside. The old woman smiles and takes the picture with her freckled hand. As she looks at it, she rocks side to side, as if she were consoling herself. She smiles again and drools a little. *That was you*, Sonia tells her. She caresses her grandmother's hand and continues perusing the album. She stops at the image of a man who is also young, almost her age. A man wearing a mustache, with a serious expression and a frowning brow that forms a deep vertical line on his forehead. A good-looking man. She can't quite accept the idea of the person in the picture actually being her father. Then the wedding—her smiling mother—and only a few more pictures—purely testimonial images of family gatherings in which everyone is posing rigidly. Old-fashioned pictures, everyone is looking straight at the camera with serious expressions, keeping their distance from each other. Next are empty spaces where the ones who shouldn't be there anymore were removed. Silences. Time periods no one has the courage to bring up in conversation. She flips through the album quickly to get to the more recent photos. The latest ones are at least four years old. One of her, holding Lucas by the hand; Elena is by her side sticking her tongue out at someone who was cropped out. Her mother and her at a birthday party. Whose? What's left of a destroyed cake, sitting on a plate over a checkered tablecloth, gives the image a grotesque quality.

She closes the album abruptly, takes the photo from her grandmother's hand, and opens a folder with forms, old receipts, cards from friends she no longer remembers. She looks at them with minimal curiosity and puts them back carelessly. She finally finds the passport picture she had taken for the internship application with the municipal archive. Her lips are pursed and she has a cold expression, but she looks attractive. She sets it aside.

The next day she scans it at the archive and sends it to Knut Hamsun along with a list of three book titles so he can pick whichever is easiest for him to get. *Thank you*, he answers. His reply is extremely brief and dry. He doesn't tell her what he thinks of the photo except that he was expecting it to be digital, not a scanned print. *But don't worry, it's as good as any. Just give me an address to get the books to you.* She explains that she doesn't have a digital camera or any digital photos. She doesn't have a computer at home. She just recently got a cell phone, the cheapest, most rudimentary model she could find—she doesn't tell him this. She also doesn't tell him that she doesn't even own a good MP3 player or decent headphones. No, she isn't about to tell a stranger her life story. She simply gives him her address and waits.

Two days later when she comes home from the archive, a compact, carefully prepared package is waiting for her. Sonia takes it to her room without saying anything to her mom, who briefly looks at her from the corner of her eye. The address on the label is written in all caps with childlike, yet clean handwriting. The sender's address is written on another label on a different side. A typical first name and a typical last name. A neighborhood in the outskirts of Cárdenas. A large number and a letter that isn't A or B, suggesting that it's a giant beehive of a building with hundreds of units. That's who Knut Hamsun is—another one of hundreds of thousands of residents in the large city.

The package obviously contains much more than what she asked for, yet she's surprised to see not three, but twelve books when she opens it. The books are neatly arranged so as not to waste any space in the box. She asked for one by Onetti, there are five by Onetti. She asked for one by Clarice Lispector, there are three by Clarice Lispector. She asked for one about dream interpretation, there are four about dream interpretation. There's also a small note. The same neat and childlike handwriting. *The shipping cost is 12.95 euro*, he writes. *Would you make me a deposit whenever you can?* An account number and a winking happy face. Lucas comes in to snoop around but she shoos him away. *Mind your own business*, she tells him. It's not easy for her to get a moment alone. She slams the door and pages through the books for a good while. She reflects on it, amazed, wonders where they come from, if they're really stolen. Nine of them have a tag from a large department store, El Corte Inglés, the rest from a large bookstore, Casa del Libro. She can't help but add it all up. Even after taking off the shipping cost, it's a substantial gift. She wonders if a pixelated file of a scanned passport photo, where her features can hardly be seen, could really be worth all that.

They continue to write to each other. But Knut Hamsun doesn't want any more pictures. At least he doesn't ask for them. Knut only wants to know about her, talk to her. First he makes contact through the books he's sent. *What did you think of* The Besieged

City? *Which of the Onetti titles did you like the most? Please, when you read it, I'd like to discuss* The Shipyard *with you.* At the end of his messages he always slips in other kinds of questions: *How old are you? Do you live with your parents? What is the place where you work like? Why did you decide to go to the get-together in Cárdenas? Did you think any of the men there were attractive?* They both stop posting in the forum—they're no longer interested in it—and they start communicating through email. Knut's come daily, are extensive, meticulously written, without full stops, and without headings or closings. Sonia notices it's impossible to end the conversations. Every reply she gives generates new questions. *Do you really think that Larsen's attraction to Galvez's wife is another proof of his disdain? Could you elaborate on why* The Body Snatcher *makes you feel unsettled? Are you really disappointed by Jung? Would you know how to explain why? Don't just say something disappoints you without elaborating. Always investigate your statements. If you don't know where they're coming from, if you can't affirm them with reasoned arguments, then you should look into them. Listen to Proust: always penetrate deeply into your intuition.*

It's much easier for Sonia to reply to the questions about her life. Yes, she does tell him she's twenty-two years old, lives with her mother, brother and sister, and grandmother. Her father died when she was a child, she can barely remember him. Her brother and sister are actually half-siblings, children of another guy who one day up and disappeared. The archive where she works is boring and plain, but at least that's where she can use the Internet to write to him. She went to Cárdenas because it was on the way, she was visiting a girlfriend. No, she didn't find any of the men at the dinner attractive; she almost never finds the men she meets attractive.

Sonia however continues without knowing much about him. A strange pride prevents her from asking. Who is Knut Hamsun really? She starts believing what he says without a shred of doubt. For example, when he claims to have the same birthday

as her. *That has to mean something!* she says. Knut believes in
destiny, he believes in God. Everything is written beforehand,
he states, including anything that can happen to them together
in the future: the matching birthday is no coincidence. In this
perfect timepiece that is the universe, everything has a reason
for being. *Sometimes I can't help staring at my hands, listening to
the noise from the street outside, and weaving together in my mind
the endless interactions that irreducibly make up our existence. In
those moments I think everything is so perfect, so wonderful, to be
alive is so magnificent . . .*

Little by little he tells her about himself, stories that Sonia
finds disjointed and, sometimes, incoherent. Knut lives with
his parents, he has no particular occupation, he left school years
ago. *Yet,* she reflects, *you know quite a lot.* What does that have
to do with anything? he replies arrogantly. It's satisfying to be
self-taught. School, he says, is the most dangerous socialization
arena. Group instruction completely annihilates the individual.
He'd rather be free. He reads and writes continually, even when
he's walking down the street. And yes, he admits, he dedicates
a significant portion of this time to the art of theft: books, but
also other goods, if necessary. He never uses the word *stealing,*
instead he says *grabbing, getting, obtaining,* and even *buying.*
Does she think it's wrong? he asks. Sonia rushes to answer no.
Adding that she thinks it's okay. She wishes she knew how to
steal books. She loves to read, but she hardly has any money.
What little she makes as an intern she gives to her mother each
month to make ends meet. She shouldn't worry, Knut replies.
Does she want more books? All she has to do is ask him.

More deliveries come in later months. Titles that she asks for,
but more than anything, titles he's suggested, or those he thinks
she should read right away. *You're the only person I know whom
I consider my equal in intellect,* he says. *The only one whom I feel
like sharing my reading with.* He takes on the role of literary

guide and she lets herself be led with pleasure. She stocks up on her new belongings, placing them in her bedroom shelf. She asks Knut to ship the packages to the municipal archive, so her mother won't get suspicious, and she brings the books home a few at a time. She enjoys the arrival of the packages, which she opens hurriedly, tearing the labels that he seems to have placed with such extreme care. One night, lying in bed, staring at the spines of the books she hasn't had time to read, she tries to find out if it's greed that's hooking her, or if maybe it's a different, more difficult-to-define drive. She admits to herself that she feels flattered. There's something enticing about his very gradual seduction through thoughtful gifts—which is gaining more and more ground. But she's confused. She actually has no particular interest in those books. She also isn't truly curious about Knut. What attracts her is knowing that she's the recipient of his attention. His way of approaching her is entirely different from any other she's experienced so far.

Obtaining books is very easy, Knut insists. *So easy that I can't stop asking myself why they aren't all looted.* He assures her that the only thing that's needed is perseverance. *Are you perseverant when you want to achieve something? When you truly want it? You often complain about your job at the archive, which you describe as frustrating or for which you are very overqualified and have a low interest level. But do you think you have strived with true perseverance to change the situation? Or have you just allowed circumstances to lead you and now complain? One must always persevere, have an ant's patience, never give up, take the necessary time to reach one's goals.* Following this premise anyone can *obtain* books or almost any other item in a large store. He does it every day, devotes his life to it, and shares part of his loot simply for the pleasure of doing so; although it's never been as satisfying to give something as it is to give to her. *Think about the joy that it brings you to open a package and find, I don't know, ten, fifteen books for you that you didn't even expect. Well that is nothing, absolutely nothing, compared to the pleasure I feel when sending them to you.*

He always charges her for the shipping costs. It doesn't make a difference if the amounts are small. If it's 4.13 euro, she deposits exactly 4.13 euro. Proud of his skill, he doesn't take the price tags off the books so that she can add it all up. The message isn't *everything he gives her* but *everything he takes for her.* All that's needed to buy things is money. To steal them, he says, other types of skills are needed.

But why me? she asks him. She doesn't give him anything in return. It can't be just for sending him a simple passport picture. Of course not, he says. The picture was the start, the trigger. It means nothing in and of itself. It isn't the picture, but the fact that she agreed to send it. It's the confirmation of an intuition. *You agreed to the first exchange without thinking about it. Where other women would have reacted indignantly, or mistrusted, you moved forward firmly.* On the other hand, it isn't true that Sonia doesn't give him anything. She writes to him, shares her opinions, tells him about her life. In return he sends her some books. It could almost be considered barter. *Taking it to the furthest extent possible, we could say that I send you books simply as payment for existing.*

Days later, a girlfriend—who she worked up the courage to tell a decaf version of the story—puts her foot down. *If you really want to know my opinion*, she said, *I think you should stop writing to him immediately.* Is it for moral reasons? Sonia asked. Did her friend think it's wrong that the books were stolen? He doesn't take them from people's houses or small bookstores, she rushed to clarify. He snags them in large stores, chains like Fnac, Vips, places like that. No, her friend said, it's not that or it's not only that. It's because no one gives gifts just because. *He wants something, and if you don't listen to me, one day this story is going to blow up in your face*, she warned. But they aren't gifts, strictly speaking, Sonia explained. There's a sort of agreement established. He likes that she writes to him, he wants to discuss books, share general opinions about life. Her friend tilts her head forward and squints her eyes slightly to look at her. *Come on,* she whispers. *Do you really think your opinions about life are worth that much?*

She also tells a male friend, although this time she exhibits a coquettish vulnerability. *Do you think it's dangerous?* she says, lowering her voice. No, he replies, pensive. He chuckles, pets her hair. *Don't be over-dramatic,* he says. Her friend finds it very noble that he steals from large department stores. After all, he explains, their wealth comes from another kind of plunder. *It's a legitimate way to re-appropriate goods that are robbed from us in the first place,* he tells her. He's curious, but only about the details: how does Knut steal?; what techniques does he use?; what does he do if he gets caught?; how much time does he devote to stealing?; how is his business structure set up?—he says *business.* If he doesn't have a job and it's true that he lives with his parents, don't they notice that he stores too many things? Don't they wonder where the stuff comes from? Sonia doesn't know how to answer. She also doesn't care too much. The minutiae don't interest her. Why look for the logical root of it? She realizes that others don't share her fascination. They don't quite get her. She also thinks they don't entirely believe her.

And if he asks her for a nude? he asks. Will she also give him one? *He's not going to ask me for that,* she laughs. *Don't be dumb.*

Have you ever been caught? Sonia asks him. *A handful of times,* Knut replies. But nothing happens, absolutely nothing. *One must not waver for that reason.* In those cases, he explains, they take you to a sort of *station,* take down your information, give you a more or less threatening little sermon and propose that you pay for the stolen thing or, if you don't have money, return

it and never show your face there again. A kind of *station?* she
asks. What exactly is this *station?* A separate room, usually small,
very dingy, where they ask you to empty your pockets or take off
your coat, so the insignificant-looking officers get a go at pretending to give the third degree to those whom they've caught
red-handed. *The whole little number is pathetic,* he assures her.
According to him, it's very easy to deceive them. He once was
caught and told them he didn't have his ID with him and made
them believe his name was Knut Hamsun. *Noot Hansin, huh?*
the intrigued guard repeated with some effort. *That's a first!* he
laughed. *But the worst is when they try to have a dialogue to help
you out of the "mistake of stealing."* Another time, when they
caught him with a pair of Salinger books in his pockets, the
guard asked him in a conciliatory tone to sit down and tell him
about Salinger. Who was that writer? Why did he want to read
him? Why was he so interested in him that he would even steal
his books? *Maybe you'll convince me and I don't have to report you
to the police,* he said. Knut replied that Salinger was a childhood
friend of his father's, a guy who had to emigrate to America and
now was successful in literature. The guard would lift his chin in
admiration as he told the story, believing every bit, even though
he had the biography on the back of the book in front of him.
*They never take it further: for them, it's enough to enjoy their small
allotment of power.*

He's been caught very few times, especially considering all
the years he's been stealing; and when he has, it's normally just
fueled his motivation. If he gets caught in one end of the city,
he goes to another to compensate for the slip. In Cárdenas,
where there are dozens of shopping malls, there's no shortage
of locations. Plus, most of the security guards, including the
undercover ones, have short-term contracts; the turnaround
is usually high. On the other hand, the veterans usually can't
remember the faces of the people they catch every day. But are
there really so many? Sonia asks, surprised. They're a legion,

he says. Every morning loads of people leave their homes to acquire items. Hundreds of them blending in here and there, invading stores like termites: books, CDs, DVDs, videogames; but also perfumes, liquor, sunglasses, food, toys, clothes. To be fair, many crumble when they're caught; they cry like babies and never try again. But many others are tenacious, they keep going, setting an example for those who are learning. There are always fresh batches of newbies willing to try it. The wheel goes round and round, never stops. *There have always been hunters and hunted, thieves and watchmen, control and chaos,* Knut affirms. *That's how the world works.*

Knut feels comfortable telling her about his expeditions. He does it in detail. He describes his favorite technique—deactivating the alarm system with special stickers—and others that exist but don't convince him—the use of pliers, magnets, freezer bags. When it comes to books, most of the time, discreetly putting them in between your clothes is enough; making sure, of course, to do it out of the cameras' range. If one follows the very subtle shine of the lenses, it's possible to know where they're focusing. Certain commercial chains also put security devices under the price tags—she can tell by feeling for a raised bump when passing her finger over it—or a thin magnetic strip inside the pages. All it takes to deactivate them is to learn which systems each place uses. Sometimes it's necessary to go in and out of the same store several times, gather the obtained goods outside of whichever shopping mall it may be—for example, inside a trash can in a low-traffic area, or in a locker at a train station. It's not possible to take eight thick books in one trip, but you can take three, then two, and then another three. It isn't that complicated if done with patience and professionalism. It's in the decisive moments when one must not fail. In Darwinian terms, he tells her, the body adapts to the tension of the situation.

He never uses his real name, although he doesn't hide it either. He doesn't sign his correspondence. His email account is under a pseudonym as well. For her, he's Knut Hamsun. Or simply Knut. The real name is nothing. It means nothing. He also never names her. Never says, *Dear Sonia*; never, *Hi, Sonia*. The messages start abruptly, exactly where the previous one left off, and always end with questions. In the beginning she thinks he's avoiding trouble in case their emails are traced. She even asks herself if she could be investigated for being an accomplice in theft. But she immediately dismisses the idea. It doesn't make sense, since the packages he sends have all his information in the sender's address. Or maybe all that is also made up?

She's never seen a picture of him. He's never made an effort to describe himself and she's incapable of imagining him. Knut is an abstraction. An abstraction that continues to periodically send her—every month, every other month—a package of books. Lately, it also comes with a record. *I get excited about sending them to you*, he excuses himself. She thanks him very enthusiastically, although she doesn't have a way to play them.

Knut's emails grow longer each time, more detailed. They include more questions, more challenges. She gets several a day, which she feels obligated to reply to, even if with two or three sentences. On occasion she makes up excuses for not writing more carefully—meetings she doesn't have, projects she isn't assigned to—but although he doesn't pressure her, her sensation of having an unpaid debt persists. Sonia asks him how he has time to write so much and at such length to her. Knut tells her he never sleeps more than two or three hours at a time. He often stays up until the middle of the night and then takes long naps during the day that allow him to stay awake the rest of the time. Many times he writes to her before dawn, so she has her email ready when she arrives to the archive. He wakes up mid-morning to see if she's replied yet. He replies immediately if so. If not, he still writes to her with more questions that he thought of in his dreams, for when she has time to reply. He insists that there's no hurry, but if there's any discussion that hasn't yet concluded, he always reminds her. *You didn't say anything about* Her *by Onetti, only that you had liked it very much, but I had asked you to elaborate. Don't forget, I am very interested;* or, *Remember that question I asked you: how do you think your life would be now if your father hadn't died?;* or, *The other day you told me that you also dream of ants, but you didn't tell me about the variations of the dream. I'd love to hear them.*

And so on like that.

It isn't only the number that surprises Sonia, it's also the way in which he expresses himself. His emails aren't improvised: they're written with conscientious effort and they're never imprecise or contain mistakes. The result, however, sounds like antiquated rambling. She doesn't tell him, but she often skims them. She tires of the rigidity, the repetition, the argumentation, and the constant persuasive tone he uses to address her. Knut tells her he always has a number of dictionaries on the table: definitions, grammar, synonyms, thesauri . . . He tells her she should get in the habit of using them too. *But they're only emails,* Sonia replies. *If I started editing everything, I would take a lot longer to reply. You're the only one reading them, it's not like they'll get published.* That is exactly why they should try to do their very best, Knut argues, because it's only for them. It's precisely in the private sphere, in the most intimate place within each of us, where negligence, passivity, and indolence must be fought.

They discuss their childhoods often. They had similar experiences. They get excited telling about their memories, as if they were trading cards. Public school. Working-class neighborhood. Pelikan pencil cases, *Sesame Street,* blue sports jackets with white stripes, La Piara ham pâté for afternoon snack. Sonia scans a childhood picture for him, hoping to get one from him in exchange where she can make out his current features. Knut limits himself to sending a fragment of his sixth-grade notebook for religion class. He has round, clean handwriting, surprisingly similar, after so many years, to that on the labels of his packages. He extends to the entire page, writing outside the margins.

I wish for a world without wars where no child is hungry.

I wish my parents live forever and never die.

I wish they would leave me alone when I am tired.

I wish the King (crossed out and replaced by *"Pope")* *a lot of happiness and for him to do good everywhere.*

Did you ever go to summer camp? she asks one day. He did, he says. He had just turned twelve. *My parents sent me to that dry, ugly, inhospitable mountain range to get me out of the way and take a trip by themselves.* He asked to go with them. He cried, begged, promised to behave. But the decision had already been made. Knut got sick a few days before; not even the fever or the vomiting made his parents' will bend. *Yes, it was a painful experience,* he says. *All of a sudden one realizes God has given one a place in the world and that it's hardly possible to change that, no matter how hard one tries.*

What he remembers most is that sex permeated everything. Or, actually, more than sex, the sexual impulse, still not understood, sad and sordid, that first contact hit him without warning, in the middle of childhood. The boys masturbated in their sleeping bags. All the time and without an ounce of discretion. There was even a camp leader who would ask them constantly if they'd already *done it,* and bragged about *doing it* every day with his girlfriend. *"You'll see, you'll see,"* he would tell them. *All I felt was disgust,* Knut tells her. *Pity and disgust. Suddenly, like through the opening of a crack, sex showed me a much harsher part of reality than I had known until then.*

He suffered terribly in that camp. He would lock himself in the bathroom stall and cry until he was exhausted. He felt a certain physical pleasure in crying that made him feel superior to the others. However, he wasn't the only one having crying fits: sometimes, when he came out, he would find other boys with red eyes. Ashamed, they avoided looking at each other.

Although fights broke out all day, what tortured him wasn't the idea of getting hit, but the possibility of his things being ruined, or simply touched. There was a rumor that the older boys would come into the younger ones' dormitories and steal whatever they wanted. Also, that they would fill their sleeping bags with toothpaste or masturbate inside of them, in front of everyone. He never saw any of that, but the rumors were enough for him to be constantly alert. It's not that he didn't have friends: it's that he couldn't trust them. Even the camp-mate he got along with the most—a quiet, reflective boy that knew how to be a good listener—ended up disappointing him on the last day. Knut was lying on his bunk bed reading when he arrived, got in the sleeping bag, and started panting. Knut didn't move his eyes away from his comic book. He blushed as the temperature rose in his face and his hands shook from indignation, but he didn't say anything. After a couple of minutes when he was cleaning himself with a sheet of tissue paper, the boy tried to explain to him why he masturbated, what masturbation meant for him. He told him that until recently he didn't do it because no cream would come out, and seeing Knut's astonished face he hurried to clarify: jizz. With a sad expression, maybe regret, he tried justifying it: to show Knut that what he was repulsed by made sense to him. But Knut didn't say a word.

He learned a lot during that camp. His innate mistrust for aggregates, ideas of totality, generalization, and uniformity, any kind of group manifestation. *I always laugh at those who claim to defend minorities, because the first minority is the individual.* Belonging to a group brings with it an inevitable moral and intellectual price that, once paid, can never be recovered. Evil is in the group's existence itself. The sense of belonging to a group always creates violence. *There are those who think that, to*

*prevent it, the solution is to expand the group as much as possible.
But some of us believe that there's no need for protection to go
through life. We do much better alone.*

After telling her the camp story, sex becomes another topic in
their emails, although with much caution. Knut admits that
he's extremely shy in that area—he says *prudish*—and Sonia
assumes this means he's still a virgin. He avoids writing certain
words, which he insinuates only with initials: f . . . s . . . c . . . He
admits that his body wants it but that his mind rejects the idea.
For him sex is an aberration: the ideal is to sneak away from the
impulse. Sonia thinks his position is fun. Aberration? Why an
aberration? Does that mean he finds her aberrant? . . . Because
she's had sex, and has sex—and thinks it's completely natural.
We aren't kids anymore, she says. No, of course not, he replies.
She's not aberrant, but the act is, however natural. *Don't make
the debate personal*, he asks. What she does is the same that everyone else does, there isn't anything special about her behavior.
He's the one who is breaking from the norm. *I suppose I am a
prisoner of something that is larger and stronger than myself, but I
want to fight it in every way I can. Sex is the most clearly distinct
aspect of a world I don't want to be part of, even if instinct acts in
the opposite direction to my will. That's why I don't have any other
safeguard than to be loyal to my childhood.*
     Sonia usually responds to his periphrases with lightness
and in a carefree style. She tells him about her first boyfriend.
Also about a Brazilian boy she loved very much but who had
to return to his country. There was a teacher who was much
older than her, married, whom she saw in secret and who
would record her with his camera when they were in bed. She
tells him about her current friend. Friend? he says. What does
friend mean? That it isn't anyone important, Sonia replies. Too
immature, too inconsistent, she adds. But what does she mean
by inconsistent, exactly? What are the ways in which he displays

his lack of maturity? Does he know he exists? What does he think of the packages? Does he think stealing is okay? Does she imagine him taking risks for her, like him, to get her a book?

Sonia thinks his jealousy is fun, she placates it, gives him a listening ear. No, of course not. He's incapable of snagging anything. She can only picture Knut doing that: the considerate, loyal, consistent, loving Knut.

On—their—birthday, Sonia receives a much larger package than usual. Her coworkers at the archive look at the box curiously; one of the women at the end of the room makes a funny comment that she can't quite hear. Sonia waits for everyone to go out for lunch to open it. She starts taking out the gifts nervously. There are books, many of them (maybe twenty?). There are CDs (ten? fifteen?). There are two notebooks, a daily planner, a box of pencils (Sonia told him recently that she loves paper and desk supplies), and there's a bottle of perfume. The expensive kind, the kind that Sonia's never been able to splurge on. She sprays some on her neck, on her wrists. The scent is heavy and enduring. Sonia isn't used to smelling like that. She isn't sure if she likes it. She hurries to put everything back in the box. It doesn't fit anymore. One of the CDs falls and the case breaks. The cover of one of the books gets folded as she shoves it back in. One of her coworkers is back, she watches from the corner of her eye. Sonia sits back down, she pretends to work on her database and the eternal, useless card indexes. She sends Knut a heartfelt thank-you message as soon as she's able. She emphasizes the perfume. He had never sent anything that personal, she says. She's moved. Knut was waiting for her reply impatiently. *I didn't sleep at all last night*, he says. *My eyelids were closing, but even then I wasn't able to get in bed, just out of pure anxiousness to see your reaction.* He's glad that she feels so happy but, she knows this, she has nothing to thank him for. Only the opportunity to chat about those books with her, he says, is more than enough to compensate the effort he made to avail himself of them. That'll be his birthday gift. They can celebrate it together that way.

He then asks her to make a deposit for the shipping costs. This time the price is 32.30 euro, he indicates. Sonia swallows saliva. It's more than she expected. It's true the package is quite heavy. It's true that the contents are much more expensive than that—the books alone are about three hundred euro. But parting with that amount of money isn't easy for her.

Even so, she doesn't dare refuse. She tells him that she will make the deposit as soon as she can.

She closes the email. Her enthusiasm has been replaced by an uncomfortable feeling of having lost control. At her feet, under the office desk, the half-open package shows the shiny cover of one of the books. The aroma of the perfume she just sprayed on herself still floats in the air around her.

2. NAP

THE RINGING OF a phone breaks the calm of the afternoon. Sonia wakes up alarmed. She hasn't gotten used to the sounds of her new home yet. Verdú lets out a groan, repositions his pillow, and mumbles something unintelligible as he turns over. Sonia gets up groggy and stumbles forward in the hallway, completely naked. Outside the room, the temperature is several degrees higher. It's mid-August; the flaming heat lurks behind the walls of the apartment. The floor is warm; the orange light filters in through the windows and the edges of the doors. She answers the call, still sleepy, rubbing one side of her face. Colored with tension, with its distinctive nervous ups and downs, the voice is perfectly recognizable to her. *It's me*, it says. *I've been calling your cell phone nonstop for days. You never pick up. Why don't you pick up my calls?*

Sonia hisses. Hang on, she says. She puts the receiver down, closes the door, and picks up the phone again. She speaks in a low voice. He can't call her there, she says. Where did he get this number? It's in the phone book, Knut answers. What phone book? What are you talking about? The phone book, the one that's always existed, he repeats. Available on the Internet. *Look it up if you want. You get a phone line and you don't even know that?*

Sonia becomes impatient. She gasps for air as she speaks. She doesn't want him to call her there, she insists. She doesn't want him to look up her phone number on the Internet. *Stop stalking me*, she orders. Knut laughs. Stalk her? That's what she would want. *Deep down you're wishing for it,* he says. He laughs again. Between a cry and a laugh, his voice cracks at times. *You feel proud just thinking about it. That way you can feel even more important, is that right? No, I'm not stalking you. I just looked up your number in the phone book! The most normal thing to do if you don't answer your cell phone! What did I do to you that's so bad you won't talk to me?* She touches the receiver with her mouth to answer. She breaks the word into syllables. *No-thing,* she says in rage. He's done nothing to her. But she has another life now. *Whatever there was between us doesn't exist anymore.* It fizzled out, she says. Dissipated, *done.* Is he not able to understand that?

Knut yells. He asks her why she grants herself the right to decide. Doesn't his opinion count? *I've given you everything for three years, and now you get rid of me like this, like I'm nothing?*

Sonia hears steps on the other side of the door and then a flush from the bathroom. *Listen,* she whispers. *I am not alone, you understand? My husband is here and he'll come any second.* Knut lets out another coarse laugh. Her husband! he says. What does that matter to him? *It's not like I am your lover. I have nothing to hide! Or is it maybe you who has something to hide?* She hurries up. She will have to hang up immediately, she says. *You have to get it through your head that I don't want to talk to you. You can't make me.*

The door opens. A head peeks through, requesting that she come back to bed please. It isn't time to answer the phone. Sonia covers the mouthpiece. *I'm coming,* she says, *I'm coming.* She's sweating. Her nostrils expand and her cheeks start flushing. She feels her own heat rise to her ears, the urgency to end the conversation immediately. She speaks into the phone again. Now it's she who yells.

Listen, she says. *You interrupted me. I was fucking him, you understand? We were right in the middle of fucking, you hear me? Can you imagine that? No? Well picture it. That's what happens when you call a phone number no one gave you. So don't call me from now on. Never. Not ever. Don't you even dare!*

She hangs up.

Verdú looks at her perplexed, framed by the outline of the door, which is now completely open. Who was that? he says stunned. How can she talk like that? Sonia comes close to him, she caresses the back of his neck. A jerk, she says. A guy she met a while ago that won't leave her alone. She apologizes. She's sorry she acted that way. Too rude, yes, vulgar, but there wasn't any other way to stop it. Forcefulness is necessary sometimes, doesn't he think?

They go back to the bedroom, to the cool sheets, the air-conditioning, the nearly shut blinds, the thin stripes of light that softly shine on the headboard. Something else, something better, Sonia thinks. They hug. Verdú laughs.

After what you said to him, I don't think he'll bother you for a long time. You were furious.

Let's hope, she replies.

An image crosses her mind, something similar to a bird with a sharp beak, wings flapping. She discards it immediately, squinting to scare it away.

They fall asleep again right away.

3. TWO YEARS BEFORE

No, I don't see myself happy, not even by your side.
Not even in the most optimistic of my fantasies do I see myself
having a happy relationship with you, beneficial for both of us:
a solid, everyday, bougie relationship. I would never quite believe
in it and I would always try to test it, to go further, until one day I
would end up violating you in some way.

THE SHIPMENTS CONTINUE. Her bedroom shelf is completely full; Sonia doesn't know what to do with so many books anymore. Her mother would find it odd if she saw them, she would try to find out how she was able to buy them. Maybe, she thinks, she would accuse her of concealing money from her. She decides to store them in a locked closet at the archive. They stay there for months without her being able to remember the titles. When Knut asks, she pretends to have read them or apologizes for not having done so yet. She also hides the perfume bottles he's gotten in the habit of including in the packages in recent months—he's sent four so far. She takes them out every now and again and sprays a little on her wrists. The smell seems too strong to her. Sonia prefers her usual body spray.

The amount you are able to read is amazing, she tells him. Knut comments extensively about Proust. He doesn't stop insisting that she should read him too, but not just part of his work, not just one book, his entire oeuvre. He suggests that they study him together, that they analyze his work in depth. *I would like nothing more in this world than that*, he says. He claims to have read *Buddenbrooks* in five days, *The Brothers Karamazov* in four. In another email he copies large segments of *Against the Grain* and asks her what she thinks of des Esseintes's views. *I sense plenty of talent in you,* he says. *If you were more consistent—and less lazy—you'd be a great writer.* Why does she think he sends her so many books? She should take the plunge and start writing, let him hold her hand as she learns, read the greats with him. He'd love to help her.

One day he asks for her phone number assuring her that he won't call. He just wants it to text her as he acquires her gifts. He sometimes feels so much excitement, he explains, that he can't contain himself and wait until the next morning to tell her. Sonia gives him her number and he in fact keeps his word and never calls. He limits himself to sending her large texts, perfectly written, without abbreviations; texts like . . . *I just obtained Pavese's diaries for you. Virginia Woolf's entire work in the bag, it's yours. Another Prince album and the* Gymnopédies *by Satie.* She thanks him but begins to insinuate that she has more than enough. *My reading speed is much slower than yours,* she says. *I hardly have time.*

Each time she feels the desire to halt the exchange more urgently, but she doesn't do anything. She incorporates Knut into her everyday life like another routine, sometimes burdensome, sometimes uncomfortable, sometimes beneficial. How hard is it to keep writing to him? she asks herself. She has hours to spare at the archive, she's bored to death. Why end it like that? Why lose everything? One doesn't meet someone like Knut every day. His intelligence. His sensitivity. His eccentricity. His generosity. His commitment; and sure, why not?, his gifts, even if she doesn't always want them. Couldn't she find a way to continue, maybe with more caution, more restraint, so the situation doesn't derail? Couldn't she at least come up with a way to have a pause for some time?

She lies that there will be restrictions on Internet use in the archive. New measures going into effect, she explains. *People abuse it here. Almost everyone spends the day online in chats, or browsing on shopping sites.* Even cases of porn-site visits have been recorded, she adds. So, the general manager called an all-staff meeting that morning and announced they'll be installing monitoring software in their computers. *I won't be able to email you for the time being,* she says. *Maybe later, when things calm down.* They've also now offered her a contract. Nothing spectacular: a temporary contract to keep doing her same absurd job, but if everything goes as planned it could be the stepping-stone to something more promising. She shouldn't be using the Internet all morning. She needs to make a good impression. As much as it pains her, they'll need to stop for some time.

The ruse doesn't work. Knut immediately proposes writing each other letters. Their relationship began thanks to the Internet, he says, but it's far beyond it. If it can't happen through email, let regular mail be the medium. The problem—the advantage, for Sonia—is that now they'll have to wait days to hear from each other. The incentive—the cost, for Sonia—is that they'll be able to reflect more—*Even more!* she thinks—about what they write and they can send each other longer letters—*Even longer!* she fears. Yet she expresses her agreement and feigns relief. *I'm glad I won't lose you,* she says.

Knut embraces the task with even more enthusiasm than before. His letters take up four, five, six double-sided sheets of graph paper: pages crowded with childlike, round-shaped handwriting, almost without any line spacing. He uses long envelopes onto which he traces the address meticulously in all caps, in the same way he does—he continues to do—for the shipments. Sonia recognizes his striving for perfection in each trace, or rather his obstinacy, the stubbornness of his constancy. His letters take very little time to arrive—there's practically one in each mail delivery—while Sonia's take as long as one or two weeks. He tells her to take her time. He feels happy just knowing that she's writing to him or that one of her letters is on its way. He often can't fall asleep wondering how much longer before the mail comes. Waiting like this leads to anxiety but he can't help it. *I'm literally overwhelmed by impatience.*

Realizing she's important to him, Sonia uses an affectionate and generous tone, yet she makes a thousand excuses for why she writes so little—one or two pages at most—and takes so long to reply. He suggests that when she's busy she write a summary of her ideas so she can develop them later; or that she write fragments periodically, as she's able, even if the end result seems a bit incoherent. The most important thing is to continue, he adds, and that they do, writing mostly about books but also about their lives—what each wants to reveal to the other. Knut focuses on his shopping-mall expeditions, filled with the usual stratagems and finales. Sonia describes her routine at the archive, her lovers, her outings—an existence she manicures to seem light, charming, and even mysterious.

The first time he mentions his physical appearance is to tell her about his tendency to gain weight. *You have no idea what it's like to always be checking the scale,* he says to her. He's 5'4" and usually weighs 165 pounds, but can weigh 176 or more if he lets himself go. Lately he's lost some weight because he hardly eats and on his pilgrimages to the malls he walks quite a few kilometers every day. His diet consists of bowls of muesli-sweetened milk, chocolate muffins, cookies, and tarts he orders from Lacrèm, a luxury bakery in downtown Cárdenas. *He doesn't eat meat and never drinks alcohol. Not for any kind of moral reason,* he clarifies. *I'm simply not interested.* He's recently gotten in the habit of going to expensive restaurants, sometimes very expensive ones, and just ordering from the dessert menu— Sonia wonders how he pays for that. He assures the confused waitstaff that he'll spend much more money this way than if he orders from the full menu. They're used to the eccentricities of their clientele, so they almost never give him any grief over it. So he sits down, orders four or five desserts—sometimes the whole list—and savors them slowly as he watches the people at other tables.

He almost always goes by himself. *I tend to embarrass my company, so I prefer it this way.* Maybe going with her would make a difference, he reflects. *Yes, I think I'd love to go with you.*

A few days before, he had been denied service in a restaurant. The noticeably uncomfortable waiter leaned in to whisper in his ear: *"Sir, we only serve normal meals in this restaurant."* He recommended the boar, the deer, the game meat. Their risottos—he mentioned, gently rubbing his palms together— were also delicious. Knut insisted that he only wanted to order desserts. This isn't a cake shop, said the waiter. *"I know it isn't a cake shop,"* Knut responded. *"They sell cakes in a cake shop. I'm here to have desserts: elaborate, restaurant desserts."* The waiter went into the kitchen to discuss it with the chef and stopped resisting Knut after he came out. They served him in the end, yes, but condescendingly. *Precisely because of that, I've promised myself to go back to that place many times.*

How much sugar does he eat? Sonia asks him. She doesn't think what he does is very healthy. It's not healthy because it isn't normal? he replies. To Knut, the healthy or unhealthy aspect is irrelevant. The only thing he's concerned about is losing control, the possibility of becoming fickle. When he feels apathetic or sad, the only thing he feels like eating is dessert. It's become an urge he struggles to fight. If he crosses the line—that is, if he stuffs himself—he resorts to self-imposed punishments. For example, as a kind of mental-resilience practice, he forces himself to button up his pants, even if they're so tight around his waist that he can't breathe fully. He also enjoys exposing himself to temptations in order to overcome them. Recently, he went to the grand opening of a fast-food restaurant where they were giving a free drink and ice cream to those who showed

up between eight and ten. He waited for about an hour in a
long line mostly made up of young people, some of whom he
thought sounded like recent immigrants. When his turn came,
he turned around to leave, but accidentally bumped into the
person standing in line behind him: a man with a Mexican
accent who took Knut's shove as a provocation and tried to
pick a fight. Raising his chin, he took a menacing posture to
challenge Knut with, *"What the hell do you stand in line and then
leave for, eh, pendejo? Just came to get your ass kicked, huh? Come
on, puto! Push me again! What's the matter? You're just a fucking
pussy, huh?"*

Knut laughed in his face, which enraged the Mexican even
more. *So he told me, as if he were dominating the situation all
along, "Yeah, thought so. You better bounce, you fucking di . . ." I
walked away victorious, not for leaving him without his fight, but
for overcoming the ice-cream temptation.*

The writing craft is another recurring subject in their letters.
Sonia should write, he repeats over and over. She should read
more and try to outline her own stories. She could start small
by trying her hand at short stories or vignettes. *You have no idea
how much I think about this*, he insists. Why doesn't he write?
Sonia asks. He reads plenty more than she does, he has more
time to spare, he'd probably be better than her. What makes him
think that she would be any good? Knut reiterates the premises
of his argument: they met in a literary forum, didn't they? She
asked for books by Onetti and Lispector, didn't she? Isn't it true
that she's written poems before? She's mentioned it to him in the
past. No, she shouldn't back out. He'll help her gain confidence.

He confesses that he frequently feels nostalgic for a time
that never existed. He's created an image of a Knut and a Sonia
who were once classmates, sitting on a lawn, trading books and
notes, like the groups of students he sees every day on university
campuses all over Cárdenas. *I don't think I would've ever adapted*

to that kind of life: schedules, rules . . . it's completely against my nature. I don't even think I would've enjoyed it, but my relationship with you is a way of making up for that existence which was never my own. The desire to share a writing project with you represents an ember of that longing.

Sonia finally goes for it and crafts a story. She writes it in one sitting, at night, nervously. Scribbling in one of Lucas's school notebooks, she narrates a chance encounter between two former classmates. Although they'd been great friends, she writes, it had been ten years since they were last in touch. Sonia tries to create a mirrored tension in the conversation—she thinks of it in those terms. They both recognize themselves in the other's slips of the tongue, in their self-betrayals; but, of course, neither of them admits it. They say goodbye in a friendly tone, feeling resentful. The story ends with a conversation one of them has in bed with his wife: *"The guy had talent,"* the character says. *"He was tenacious, determined, ambitious even. But when you see him now, when you see where that's gotten him, you realize all his efforts to achieve were worthless. Youth is overrated. It doesn't matter what we choose. Everything is predetermined somehow."*

Now you'll realize why you shouldn't have such high hopes for me, Sonia jokes when sending it to Knut.

Her excitement deflates when she gets his comments. The story is great, he says. It doesn't disappoint him at all. What's more, it confirms one by one all the predictions he's made about her. However, he'd like to point out a *major flaw:* the entire point of the story is to create the effect of the final phrase. Couples don't talk like that, especially before going to sleep. Further, he doesn't understand what she means by reflecting that *"everything is predetermined."* Did she choose the phrase because of how it sounds? Or for its supposed depth? Because he just doesn't see it. It doesn't make any sense to him. He outlines further observations: *that use of "relates" on page 2 is incorrect. A scene can't be related, it's what's said (a conversation, etc.) that gets related. On page 3, you say "He couldn't remain silent due to it."; a better way of saying would be, "it was why he couldn't remain silent." And you need to fix a repetition, "WITH the hope of alternating WITH a classmate."* He also criticizes her excessive rhetoric. He thinks she wrote empty, unnecessary sentences. She abuses the metaphor as a resource: a sign of a poorly focused literary style, he tells her. She's copying models, which only results in her voice being drowned. *Remember what Proust said: when we take on writing we should sacrifice the style of the works we love for the unique truth that exists only within ourselves.*

She should read Herbert Lottman's biography of Flaubert. He'll include it in his next shipment. *We'll discuss it,* he says. *I won't let you get discouraged. Although you may not think so, this has been a good start. You have no idea how thankful I am. Remember: one day all you'll get is praise, and when that day comes, you shouldn't forget I was the first one to see your worth.*

Sonia feels the burn of humiliation for days.

Why doesn't she take notes when she reads? How has she not finished *Le Grand Meaulnes* yet? But it's only three hundred pages without the prologue—and she started it three weeks ago! How about they discuss Richard Ford's stories in the meantime? She read them a couple of months ago and hasn't shared any of her observations. Sonia tells him she'd love to but that she doesn't remember the stories that well anymore. *I am so forgetful!* She tells him about the times she's started to read a book and realized thirty or forty pages into it that she's already read it. Knut shares his surprise. She read Ford's stories two months ago and has already forgotten them? Unbelievable! She shouldn't excuse herself by citing a bad memory. It's not a matter of *good* or *bad* memory. It's about will and effort. Memory isn't a divine gift. It's cultivated through discipline; if one wants it, one has it. *Remember what Proust tells Céleste Albaret: The true journey starts with memory.* It's precisely for that reason one must never neglect it. *Just now, for example, I didn't know where the diacritical mark went in "Céleste." I had to get up to go look it up. Today I'll try to mentally repeat to myself that it goes on the first "e."You might think it's silly, that it's unnecessary to be such a perfectionist, that it's impossible to know how every single name is spelled and that, ultimately, who cares? But it's an exercise in tenacity. The opposite attitude is the most prevalent one: to be swept along. And, yes, fickleness has a lot to do with it; with not remembering what one's done. I suppose this is the way you forgetful people protect yourselves against the harsh realities of the world.*

Knut writes down all his thoughts. If he lost his journal, he would die. It's a shame that she doesn't do anything to correct herself and improve. *You have brilliant ideas but, because you forget them too easily, you're incapable of making connections between them. Follow Tolstoy's advice: before falling asleep, remember everything you've done that day, recall each detail.* This practice may lead to obsessiveness, but that will always be preferable to amnesia.

The night before, he cites as another example, he had forgotten something that had been on his mind since summer. It involved two parts: one with three pieces of information, and a second with two. *Not five, but three plus two, which is utterly different.* He was missing a piece from the group of three. That gap in the mental series tortured him, he felt it as a personal failure that could destroy him. *Emptiness, in the most terrifying sense of the term,* he said. He spent the night trying to recall it. He fell asleep at three, woke up at five, and by eight thirty he hadn't gotten up; he was so tired, he couldn't muster the strength, not even to use the restroom. He got back in bed mid-morning and began to force his memory muscle again, until he fell asleep from exhaustion. When the afternoon rolled around, he still hadn't remembered the missing piece of information. Its absence was tormenting him more each time he tried. So he lay down—he tells her—tried concentrating on remembering the moment he first thought of it—a cool Saturday night in an empty subway car, almost a *film noir* scene. He started thinking insistently of the other four pieces of information—two from the first part and two from the second— but his mind wandered immediately and he had to fight to bring back his attention. *I can spend hours like this, one after another, feeling the resulting pain. Truly, I can't understand how you can speak so joyfully about your forgetfulness. Forgetting something is a legitimate agony to me.*

Yes, he's stressed, he admits; but he can't imagine a reality in which he could escape his nerves. *Every health issue I've had throughout the years is due to stress—folliculitis, pimples, urgent need to use the restroom, swollen gums, trouble sleeping. I often feel like I'm about to have a breakdown.* Stealing is a remedy for him. He's able to neutralize all these negative symptoms by putting his tension into the service of theft. His success in stealing owed most definitely to eliminating or minimizing the contingency of error by being methodical and obsessive, to double-checking the details more than a thousand times: that nobody's looking, that there aren't any incognito security guards, that the cameras aren't focusing on him, that the alarm systems are properly de-activated. *One of the joys of theft is that, like in gambling, you are able to face your anxiety whether you win or you lose. When you can't bear your anxiety anymore, your only option is to take action: it's a form of catharsis.*

People with fixations like checking to make sure they've closed the window, that they haven't forgotten the keys, that they've turned off the heat or the faucet—he explains—are really just trying to regain a lost sense of safety, to confirm that the universe is still in order. *The thought of the unknown future usually terrifies me; I try to immediately resolve what's within my reach—perhaps arm's reach is the most accurate way of putting it— so that I can at least know those loose ends are tied up.*

I met someone. She tells him a few months after. *Someone I really like.* She's not making it up. His last name is Verdú. She calls him Verdú, everyone does. *He's outgoing, affectionate, fun, and has this way of approaching everything with simplicity that's so charming.* Sonia spares no effort complimenting Verdú whenever she mentions him. Knut immediately shows interest. What does he do? he asks. Where did she meet him? He's a biologist, she explains. He works in an ornithological research station, he puts leg bands on birds, feeds chicks, takes excrement samples, *that sort of thing,* she summarizes. They were introduced by mutual friends at a peace protest. They got along immediately. They talked about a whole host of subjects and share almost all opinions. Verdú called her to get together the next day and, after a couple of beers, they kissed right there at the bar, sitting on the barstools. Sonia is euphoric. She confesses that although it may seem like it's too soon, they're planning on moving in together.

Knut's reaction is cold at the beginning but quickly turns abrasive. She met him at a protest? Since when does she go to protests? He imagines it was one of the many against the war with whichever Asian country is supposed to be the enemy now. *Oh yeah, here in Cárdenas people too have taken to the streets to join the plight for a more just world,* he says with irony. Does she feel like a better person for chanting antiwar slogans? He considers protests a complete waste of time. She already knows what he thinks of any sort of group endeavor. *Ah the pressure of the group . . . it's pure dictatorship.* But what he's most concerned about is her sudden infatuation. *Have you read Proust's thoughts on the matter?* he asks; and then goes on to censure her with, *ultimately the philosophy you are operating under is just like* Cosmo *magazine's—exactly the same.* She should realize that she'll eventually see all the qualities she's now attributing to this Verdú guy in other men. Love isn't more than a projection of our own shortcomings, it's an unreality, like Odette and Albertine were for young Marcel. The idea of living together—*"as a couple"*—may seem good, but in her case it sounds more like an escape from her family than legitimate independence. Sonia is getting out of one prison to enter another. *True independence can be achieved only by living alone.* The only thing Sonia is seeing in Verdú is the opportunity to escape. Knut perceives it exactly like that, and he expresses it to her just so, with that degree of harsh detachment.

Sonia interprets his reaction as jealousy. She understands it but feels attacked. So, she attacks in return. She resents lessons on independence from someone who lives with his parents, who doesn't work, who doesn't do anything. She resents him accusing her of being opportunistic because what she feels for Verdú is authentic. She resents that he trivializes the antiwar protests when hundreds of innocent people are dying. Or is he in favor of war? Does he not care about the killing of children? The images of their small bodies, completely ravaged, appear in the news every day. How can he be insensitive to that?

Knut's perfectly organized, point-by-point response follows. It's true that he doesn't work but that doesn't make him less independent. While Sonia is subject to the group's impositions—so deepseated that she isn't even aware of their existence—he is free. His theft practice is probably the most tangible proof. *Having a job doesn't mean anything. The only thing having a job is good for is to keep having a job. I don't have a job, that's correct. I'm devoted to acquiring things and contemplating the universe, which is not a small task.* In the end, what's the difference? He gets all the things that she gets with her salary much more easily by skipping the chain of command of the bourgeois system. She's much more dependent and, of course, much more conservative, regardless of what protests she goes to. *Even if you lose your voice chanting antiwar slogans, I don't think you're more of a pacifist than I am.* And no, he never called her an opportunist, did he use those words? *Opportunistic?* No. He limited himself to saying that, to her, Verdú seems like *an opportunity*, which is substantially different. *Oh that subconscious . . . Could it be that it's you who's feeling a little . . . opportunistic?*

Regarding the war, yes, he is concerned about the death of children; but he's concerned in the same measure Sonia is. No more, no less. *It's just that I don't go around announcing it. I think about it for a moment, I find it awful, and then I forget about it. Like you do. Like everyone does. Or are you losing sleep every night over those children?*

In Cárdenas, he tells her, McDonald's, Burger King, and Starbucks are busier than ever on protest days. *All the people who argue multinational corporations represent the most atrocious form of capitalism stuff themselves with burgers and cappuccinos in paper cups, but then go out and chant pacifist slogans. If you were to steal their cell phones, there probably isn't one of them who wouldn't berate you, hit you, or think it's fine if you are tortured in the police station. Try stepping on one of them in one of your marches and you'll see that it bothers them more than all the mutilated children in the world.* He admits to being much more ashamed by garbage on the street than by the existence of nuclear weapons, for instance. The scale of his concerns starts with the individual and then, way over at the other end, incorporates the collective. *But I don't say this to convince you of my views or anything like that. If you don't want to know my opinion, by all means just say it. I'll happily oblige.*

She folds the sheet of graph paper and puts it back in the envelope. She feels an anxious tingle in her stomach. Who has time for this? she thinks: I'm tired of it. She sees her copy of *The Captive* sitting on the bed next to her, with half of the bookmark sticking out. She picks it up, reads two pages, then carelessly puts it facedown, accidentally folding the edge of a page. She texts Verdú; gets an answer; texts again; new answer. A place and time. She thinks for a few moments. *OK,* she replies. *See you there.* After the exchange she starts dozing off; but her mother's voice, calling from her grandmother's room, scares the feeling of slumber away.

Come give me a hand!

Sonia and her mom manage to pick her grandmother up from her bed and sit her down on an old worn-out armchair. Lucas is jumping around in the room. Sonia rubs her chin with a concerned look on her face.

Her nightgown got crumpled underneath, she's going to get chafed.

It'll be fine, her mother says. *She's absolutely fine.* She comes close to Sonia and gently grabs her arm. That hair! Sonia thinks. Why doesn't she do a goddamned thing about that awful, frizzy hair of hers already? *Please stay here this afternoon,* her mother asks. Lucas's teacher called this morning. She has to meet her at his school. She told her he hasn't been turning in his homework lately and he's started hitting some of his classmates. *He's behaving aggressively, like he's angry about something. That's what the teacher said. We can't ignore it.*

We? Sonia thinks. *Don't make me part of this,* she protests. She straightens her posture and takes her mother's hand off her arm. She can't stay there all the time, she tells her. One day she'll move out, she'll live somewhere else, she has the right to live her life. Then what? What will she do? Does she think she can stop her?

We're a family! her mother yells.

Lucas stops jumping. He turns around quickly to look at them and smiles. His teeth are shining. *I want a dog!* he cries out. Sonia feels a hole in her chest, the sudden need to break or tear something. She leaves the room without saying anything. No, she thinks. You're not a family, you're dead weight, you're a clamp, a cage. She remembers what Knut wrote about Verdú.

Escaping the cage.

She can hear her grandmother, who's started singing in a faint voice, out of tune. The slow melody becomes almost inaudible, drowned out by the insistent rhythm of a pneumatic drill hammering mercilessly on the street outside. Sonia races down the stairs. She stops at the door, looks down, and notices how old her shoes are. The drill also stops for a few seconds, then continues; this time louder than before, as if the volume were regulated by her rage. Sonia steps outside and sees a man drilling on the sidewalk. He seems focused on his task. He's not wearing a shirt. The sun shines on his entire back. He's sweating.

She starts to calm down as she makes out the details of his appearance. She climbs up the stairs again, dragging her feet to reach each step. One, two, three. She counts them as she goes. Forty-four, forty-five, forty-six, and done.

She doesn't even know why she keeps writing to Knut but she does. In fact, she excuses herself for taking so long to reply. Yes, she feels discouraged by his last words, which she considers an unjustified attack. She often has the feeling that he's kidding. Is his statement about being more concerned by garbage than by nuclear weapons serious? When he says things like that, she doesn't know what to say. But it's not only that. It's that . . . what can they talk about now? She already knows his opinion about her relationship with Verdú. And books, well it's not really a good time to discuss books. Maybe she'll disappoint him by saying this, but she hasn't been reading or writing lately. With so many new things going on, she hardly has a moment. So, really, she doesn't see the point in writing each other right now. Why don't they at least take a break?

Her letter barely fills half a page. She writes a dry goodbye.

Why stop? Knut replies. *I don't want to stop. What I would like is to understand the reasons for your contradictions. The more I think about it, the less I do. It's not that your attitude disappoints me— disappointment is not the right word—it's that I can't picture where the time constraint is coming from.* The only new thing in her life, according to what she says, is Verdú. *Don't try bringing up your mother, your grandmother, or your work. The rest is the same as before.* And if he were to take that logic further, Verdú doesn't represent a change either, because there were others before him. The fact is that she doesn't read or write. She's joined the ranks of those who believe literature is a disposable form of entertainment that isn't worth their time when better things in life come up. *Verdú also thinks it's a hobby, am I right?*

And no, he never jokes. When he tells her he's tormented by filth, he's completely honest. He figures this aversion has to do with one of his neuroses. He's had the habit of constantly checking the soles of his shoes since he was a boy. In restaurants, he thoroughly inspects each utensil before using it; he gets up to wash his hands two or three times during the meal, and one more time after he's finished eating. He often has nightmares of clogged or overflowing toilets. The other night, he'd also dreamed of cleaning under his bed: removing mounds of iron-filing, wet sheets of paper, and some sort of putty. He could almost feel his throat burn from breathing in the minute, metallic-tasting flakes through his mouth. He woke up coughing and gagging. Filth bothers him almost at a metaphysical level. When he walks by a street frequently enough to notice that no one sweeps it, he feels that life is worthless. *I couldn't care less about chemical weapons, but when I see garbage where it doesn't belong, all I can think of is the end of our existence.*

Sonia takes off to Paris with Verdú for a few days. She writes a summary for Knut when she comes back, as if she were obligated to keep him updated. She discloses that she's decided to get married. Why not? It'll be a small wedding, they don't need to impress anyone. The trip to Paris was modest as well. They stayed in a family inn, on the outskirts of the city, and survived on kebabs. *Thank God sitting by the edge of the Seine was free,* she adds. *Don't take this personally, but I'm starting a new life.*

Knut mocks her trip in his reply. His handwriting looks slightly more rushed this time. Nervous strokes form sharp pointed letters and etch the sheets of paper. He'd rather never leave his neighborhood in Cárdenas than travel to Paris like that, he tells her. *You won't admit it, but you know going there to end up eating kebabs near the Seine is ridiculous. Did you imagine you'd smell a hint of L'Air du Temps? Did going to Fnac make you feel sophisticated? I suppose you also now feel that a croissant in any café in Paris is better than anywhere else in the world. Please! Don't be so ordinary!*

He assumes that, "with so much going on," she still hasn't started writing. *Didn't you take your little Moleskine notebook to collect fragments of inspiration like everyone else? It's truly sad to hear you're wasting your time like this, happily headed nowhere.* But he won't let that discourage him. He's recently acquired Cheever's complete short-story collection, as well as new editions of three of his novels. He'll go to the post office to mail them to her in a few days, along with a couple of CDs. *If it isn't too much of an inconvenience, text me to let me know if you're interested in anything else so I can fill up the box.* He ends the letter without a goodbye or signature, without any kind of closing.

She looks out her open bedroom window. Two dogs bark furiously at each other. They yank at their leashes with all their strength while their respective owners pull on them to hold them back. Their loud, high-pitched growling thunders in the air. Sonia notices an elderly woman who starts walking in their direction, shuffling her espadrilles very slowly, barely moving, as she pushes a rickety shopping cart forward. When the woman finally reaches the dogs, she passes them with indifference and they suddenly become silent. The owners relax, regain control of the situation, and start walking in opposite directions.

Several tourist brochures cover Sonia's desk. The northern coast. Charming towns nested between the ocean and the mountains, wooden houses, nature. Still so much left to do, she thinks. She closes the window, picks up the phone, and slowly dials a number. She hesitates, checking it against the digits printed on an official document. A bureaucrat with a thick northern accent answers the call.

. . . *We'll still need the birth certificates, you tell me.*

Sonia babbles at first, caught off-guard. *They . . . They're on the way,* she finally says.

And the copy of the witnesses' IDs?

That won't take long.

She can't tell if the man has just burst into laughter or if he's started coughing.

Can I ask you why you're getting married all the way up here?

Sonia doesn't respond. She thanks him for his help and says goodbye.

She calls the inn and then talks to a friend.

. . . *No, no, something simple . . . just at the court . . . no ceremony . . . two random witnesses . . . no, no suits, no family, no crazy expenses . . . just a weekend . . . he, he, he, yes . . . we'll stuff ourselves with seafood, just the two of us! . . . my mom? . . . no, nothing yet, no . . . yeah . . . Lucas more than anyone . . . I'm sure she'll miss me . . . then back home . . . yeah, absolutely . . . no doubt . . . a new life . . . I'm hoping . . .*

She likes to repeat that expression lately. She uses it in conversation whenever she can, as if she were seeking approval, or some sort of confirmation: *a new life.* She switches between feeling guilty and excited. The walls in her house seem to have been slowly eating away at her life.

Knut's latest letter is forgotten under the pile of brochures. It isn't a concern at the moment.

The calls begin. The first one comes at night. Sonia had stayed up late. When she hears the phone vibrate on her nightstand, she turns over to look at the screen, groggy. His blinking name flashes in her dark room. She lets it ring again and again until he gets tired. Next comes a text message. He asks her to call. He says, *please.* The tone is urgent. Sonia doesn't do it. Two or three more calls come in the next couple of days, several messages—his tone goes from supplicating to aggressive. She doesn't answer those either. She doesn't hear from him for a few days after that, until one more text message arrives when she's at her desk in the archive.

The last shipment is pending. You didn't tell me if you wanted anything else. So, I'll send you what I have. I can't keep it for you until you feel like answering.

Sonia stops to think for a moment. There's ringing in her ears. It's just stress, she tells herself. Two more days before she leaves home. Everything is rushed and complicated. Why does it always have to be like that? she wonders. The ringing subsides. She takes her phone and stares at it for a moment before quickly typing, *Why don't you leave me alone?* A loud buzz catches her attention: insect wings fluttering erratically somewhere close by. She looks up and squints, trying to find out where the noise is coming from. Her coworker watches her disapprovingly, with a half-smile. Sonia rereads the message, erases it, and changes it to, *Why do you want to keep sending me gifts?* The buzzing gets louder and faster. *Do you hear that?* she asks her coworker, holding her phone with her thumbs raised and flexed. *Hear what?* her other coworker says. No, no, she erases the text again. She can't ask him anything. If she asks a question, she's doomed. There will be an answer and then another question and it'll start all over. She has to give him an order, cut-and-dried. *Don't send me anything. I don't want anything.* OK. That's better. She sends the message. The noise stops.

Knut calls her immediately. He calls three times in a row. She takes the third call and walks out to the hallway. She's surprised by a raspy, dissonant voice with some female-sounding overtones. He's definitely upset. She hears an unstoppable, torrential downpour of words. Is he yelling? Maybe this is his normal tone of voice. Actually, yes, he's speaking loudly, she realizes. He seems nervous, very nervous. He calls her *ungrateful.* She pulls the phone away from her ear. She walks further down the hallway. He keeps talking without taking a breath. Why is she treating him like this? What did he do to earn her disdain? Is she refusing the package to prove that she hates him? She manages to interrupt him by yelling. No, she says. She has more than enough books. She has more music than she can listen to in months. She has enough perfume to last for that long too—especially since she hasn't worn it—although she doesn't tell him this. *We're obviously not on the same page. We'll never be. Why continue?* She doesn't want him to bother shopping for her sake anymore, she doesn't want him to waste his time treating her to things, or risk getting caught for something she didn't even ask for.

What do you care? he insists. *You don't mind humiliating me when you don't answer the phone and now you're worried I'll get caught stealing?*

Always that questioning tone, Sonia thinks. First in the letters and now over the phone. Always advancing through interrogation. The inflection of his voice adapts to each question, screechy, discordant, rising and falling as he emphasizes the words. Why are they not on the same page? What does she mean by that? Can she explain it in more detail? Is disagreeing on an issue—the antiwar protests, the kebabs or whatever—reason enough to leave behind an almost three-year relationship? Is that her idea of being a pacifist? Of building consensus? Of dialogue? Of course there's Verdú, but there have been others, and there will be others. With how many has she exchanged letters like she has with him? And what advantage does she see in not accepting shipments anymore? Does she think it'll make her more decent, nobler? Is it pride? Does she really not want the Cheever books? He can't understand what she gains by rejecting them. If she doesn't have time, she doesn't have to read them now. She can keep them and read them later.

A coworker is looking at Sonia with curiosity in the hallway. Sonia walks away from him toward the stairs. She turns left, and walks down a few steps. Once she's alone again, she takes a deep breath and replies, cutting: *When I want to read those books, I'll buy them myself. It's my final word.* Knut stops talking for a few seconds. She can hear the agitation in his breath. *Have you thought of buying them from me?* he finally says. *I think it's completely stupid for you to spend all that money. If not accepting the gifts is a matter of dignity for you, I can sell them to you at half price.*

Sonia sighs, annoyed. Will he never understand what she's saying? Doesn't he realize he's bothering her?

Knut laughs. A breathy laugh, it almost sounds like choking. *Unbelievable*, he says. *So now I'm a stalker. Who knows? I may even be harassing you. Is that really how you see me?*

Sonia hangs up. Her hands are shaking. She goes back to her desk, turns off her phone, and faces it down on the desk without looking at it. Her coworker points at the floor. *You were right*, she tells her. *It was a bug. It was burning inside the lamp.* On the tile, a grasshopper twitches a few last times, dry, dying. Sonia gets up and steps on it without showing any sign of disgust. *Poor thing*, she whispers.

She watches the landscape go by through the car window. Drought-stricken fields. The sun's mirage on the highway. The rhythm created by the distance between the telephone poles. The north approaching slowly, revealing that it too may just be an illusion, an imagined future on an unreachable horizon. Sonia has a bitter taste in her mouth. She sits in the passenger side, pensive, licking her teeth over and over.

Is this the right thing to do? she asks herself.

Her phone starts ringing when they reach the tollbooth.

She silences it before the first ring ends. Verdú is busy getting change and she thinks he doesn't notice. He later gives her an inquisitive look. She shrugs her shoulders. *I never pick up if I don't recognize the number. It's always telemarketers.*

Between settling into their new home and her moving out of her mother's apartment—including her mother's surprise, the bleeding wound caused by Sonia's sinful abandonment, *I can't believe you didn't trust me, Sonia. You should've told me before*—the fast move was constantly interrupted by Knut's calls, which went on for days, until he seemed to finally give up.

A week after Verdú and Sonia had installed their new landline, on the day they were taking their first nap together in the new place, one last call came through. This would truly be the last. *Listen*, she said. *You interrupted me. I was fucking him, you understand? We were right in the middle of fucking, you hear me? Can you imagine that? No? Well picture it. That's what happens when you call a phone number no one gave you. So don't call me from now on. Never. Not ever. Don't you even dare!*

Sonia is home alone when the mailman arrives. The package weighs over ten pounds. It seems to be gift-wrapped, but when she looks closely, she realizes the wrapping paper is actually a montage: hundreds of little photocopied pictures of an old man's face are repeated across the sheet—gray hair, puffy skin, and large bags under the eyes. Knut's signature labels are handwritten with capitalized, block-print letters, this time with her new address, which he must have also gotten from the phone book. The mailman hands her the confirmation slip. *You got quite the gift there, I'm gonna be sore tomorrow just from carrying it up the stairs.* Sonia thanks him, signs the slip, and struggles to drag the box across the living room. She tears the mailing tape with a pair of kitchen scissors. The first things she sees, packed on top of everything else, are the Cheever titles. Underneath she finds many more books, a number of dictionaries, and a few CDs. Some books are writing manuals—*How to Write Short Stories, Narrative Techniques, The Writer Within*—one is about ornithology. He also includes two bottles of perfume. A handwritten note at the very bottom reads, *I swear this is the last one. The shipping cost is 14.50 euro. The one about the little birds is a gift for my friend Verdú if you allow me the pleasure.* Sonia looks at the price tag: 85 euro. Beautiful color photography, high quality printing. A great gift. An obvious joke, in his usual dark humor. She rushes to put it all away. A few more books won't be noticeable. There's still room in the new dining-room shelves. The CDs are not a problem either, but the thick dictionaries will be. She shoves them, along with the bottles of perfume, in a gym bag in the back of a closet. What about the box? She has to hurry. She uses the scissors to cut it up in smaller pieces and goes downstairs to throw them in the recycling bin outside. She finds herself staring at the wrapping paper. She tears a piece right before coming back upstairs and puts it in her pocket.

During dinner she shows it to Verdú, who inspects it for a few seconds.

He looks really familiar, he finally says. He chews his food slowly, still thinking. He gets a sudden bright look in his eyes. *Oh, I know! It's that guy from the big department stores . . . El Corte Inglés. It's Isidoro Hernandez, the owner or the CEO, I can't remember. He looks pretty stupid in that picture. Ha, imagine being a billionaire and having that face.*

Sonia smiles.

Why do you have it?

She's caught off guard. *What?*

How come you have the picture?

Oh, no reason. She hesitates. She found it in the street, she tells him. It just caught her attention.

They both stare at the torn-off piece of paper sitting on the table. Verdú starts chuckling. *It caught your attention? Why would anyone be interested in that?*

Sonia shrugs her shoulders.

Why not? I am. She smiles. *I have a gift for you by the way. I'll give it to you after we clean up. It's a bird book. I got it on sale. It's written for laypeople but I think you'll like it.*

He takes her hand and kisses it.

I'm sure I will.

4. DOG

So, you basically ignored my advice.

Sonia's friend squints, giving her a severe look. *You kept writing him and he kept sending you stuff.*

Sonia smiles to herself and slowly nods. She gestures with her hand toward the shelves. *Lots of these books and CDs.* She lowers her voice. *Almost all of them, to be honest.*

It's impossible not to remember him. There's a gift from him everywhere I look. She gets up and takes out a book from one of the shelves.

Look at this. Bilingual edition; with lithographs. Limited print. It's at least a hundred euro.

And you need that because . . . ? Have you actually read it?

She puts the book back.

No. I haven't even opened many of the books; and I'm not sure I'll ever read them.

Why did you take them, then?

Sonia responds hurriedly, alternating with silences, hesitations, and looking away at times.

I didn't ask for them. I did at some point, a couple of times, in the beginning; but he immediately started sending me books according to his interests, like following a set plan. What he thought I should read. The same with the records. It was what he thought I should listen to. We then had to comment on everything. Sometimes we'd have really interesting conversations. I learned some things from him. He claimed that I had literary talent; that if I really wanted to, if I took it seriously, he could coach me to produce something worthwhile. He would also say he was proud to be the first one to recognize it. But sometimes, most of the time, writing to him felt like a chore. An obligation. Because he was so . . . She hesitates in silence as she searches for the word. *Exhaustive. That's it. So exhaustive. You had to analyze every detail to converse with him. You couldn't just go with a simple impression. You had to delve deeply into it, rationalize it all, perfectly explain the smallest things. It would bother him if you didn't keep up with his pace. He wouldn't say it directly but he would find a way to show his disappointment. When everything between us seemed to be going well, he would have the need to put pressure, to test me, he would even get aggressive. I'd eventually get tired of it and create distance. But later I'd feel guilty and come back.*

But you didn't answer. Why did you take the gifts if you weren't interested in them? What was the point?

Sonia comes back to sit on the couch, she interlaces her hands behind her head, and sits back, thinking.

I don't know. Partly to not let him down, I guess. To not hurt his feelings. He seemed so excited to send them to me . . . How could I reject them? It would've been cruel. I think I also took them out of . . . She stops for a few seconds. *Vanity. It's tempting to be the center of someone's attention in such an extreme way. Imagine a guy that gives you all that, like it's nothing. Just because. Without asking for anything in return. Simply because he wants to treat you. Because you take it. That's it: only because you are there to receive it.*

Wow, Sonia. I don't get it, really . . . I'd never let anyone . . . She lowers her voice and looks for the boy in the living room out of the corner of her eye. He's on his knees near the hallway, making a tower out of wooden blocks.

I mean, that stuff is stolen, Sonia. That didn't matter to you?

Sonia shrugs her shoulders and sips her drink.

Honestly, no. It wasn't an issue I would ponder. He didn't break into private property demanding books, he didn't threaten helpless old ladies with a knife to take their Prousts and their James Joyces.

*It's ridiculous to think of it in those terms. He just went to large
department stores, huge commercial chains. Those big multinationals
were hardly losing anything. He wasn't harming anyone.*

Her friend sighs.

Can you really steal that much stuff every day, like that?

Apparently, you can.

*Do you think maybe he was sick? What's it called? Like, that he's
a kleptomaniac?*

Of course not. Please. No, not at all.

The blocks make a loud noise as they fall on the floor. The
boy gets up and starts to whimper. He runs to Sonia and hugs
her legs.

It's OK, honey. She caresses the back of his neck. *It's OK.*

*Mommy will help you make another tower. We'll build an even
bigger one together, won't we?*

He's almost two, isn't he?

Next month . . . He's growing so fast.

Sonia gives him a kiss and gently wipes away the tears. He
walks back to his corner. Her friend readjusts her posture on the
couch and looks up. She zeroes in on the thick layer of dust on
the ceiling lamp for a second.

*Didn't you wonder if he was lying? What if they actually weren't
stolen goods? Maybe he was just a loaded guy who got obsessed with
you and bought you all those things.*

Sonia wets her lips and shakes her head.

*No, that would be absurd. Why would he tell me they were stolen
if he bought them? It doesn't make sense.*

*I mean, nothing about it makes sense, Sonia. Really. Think about
it. It's hard to believe he didn't ask for anything in return other than
a passport photo. He even gave you perfume.*

What are you saying? Sonia raises her voice.

The boy stops moving, his hand freezes right before placing a
wooden block on his new tower. He turns his little head to look
at her.

Oh c'mon, don't get upset. I'm not insinuating anything. I'm just surprised. He didn't want to meet you? He never asked you out? Did you at least talk on the phone? I know, I know. I'm asking too many questions. I'm sorry. It's just confusing, that's all. You say you didn't even see a picture of him but got letters from him every day? Were you really not curious? That sounds so strange to me.

Hey, believe me, I get it. Sonia interjects. *Do you want another drink? It'll take me a while to tell you the entire story.*

She hears her son stutter while she twists the ice-cube tray in the kitchen. Her friend is asking him a question but can't understand his answer. The child gets impatient. He repeats the same phrase more loudly each time. Sonia's breathing becomes agitated. She doesn't want to go back to the living room yet. She takes a sip of her drink and looks out the window over the kitchen sink. She can see a large mound of brown hair in the neighbor's courtyard.

Hey . . . There you are . . . Poor thing.

A very large dog raises its head and looks at her with moist, supplicating eyes. The sound of its tail thumping against the cobblestone bothers her to the point that she gets a burning feeling in her throat.

You poor thing. How can they keep you in there?

The dog extends its paws in front of its body, lowers its head, drooling. Sonia watches as she takes sips and whispers, *Poor thing.* She pours herself a refill and closes the window before coming back to the living room. The boy, now sitting next to her friend on the couch, is still trying to get his message across.

He's telling you he made the tallest tower ever with his dad yesterday. Right, love?

Sonia puts the two glasses on the coffee table and watches the soft movement of the floating ice cubes for a few instants. *C'mon, honey. Go back to play.*

The boy trots back humming to his tower.

Sonia leans back on the couch.

Do you think I drink too much?

Jeez, Sonia. You're asking me?!

Sometimes I think so. I don't know what "too much" is supposed to be, though. You know? How much am I supposed to drink? I don't know if you can drink the same way when you live on your own or with someone, when you're free, or when you have a stable job and a child to take care of. Lots of women my age . . . You, even . . . I don't know. She shakes her head. *They're such different lives.*

Her friend giggles.

Ah, you're going on a tangent. You want to change the subject, don't you?

No, not at all. I was about to tell you to ask me anything. I'm an open book.

So, you haven't told Verdú. Right?

Of course not. If you don't even understand it, you think he—of all people—would? I know it's hardly believable. But it happened. It really happened. I didn't dream it.

They take a few sips in silence. Her friend looks at her from the corner of her eye. Sonia drums her fingers rhythmically on her cocktail glass. She's swaying a little. She doesn't seem to notice. She starts speaking in a weak voice after a minute. She's starting to slur her words and her voice cracks at times.

He had an extraordinary mind. He had no choice but to act that way. He was out of the norm in every way. That's what I think. He behaved like he did because he needed to escape normalcy. Imagine being born with that brain and having only that to fall back on. You have this profound mind and everything around you is banal and vulgar. Your only choice is to reject everything, sabotage it from the inside, destroy it. He even rejected his name . . . a normal name, the name of, I don't know, millions of people? He went by a different name. Did I tell you that?

She clears her throat before continuing, puts down the empty glass and starts speaking with a hazy look in her eyes.

Knut Hamsun, a Norwegian writer from the first half of the twentieth century. One of those who was relegated to oblivion because he supported the Nazis. He didn't particularly like his writing that I know of. He never talked about his books. He never told me why he took his name. Maybe because he was a cursed writer, someone who was considered abominable, an outsider, a weirdo, who knows?

He liked to flirt with those kinds of things. He'd hang out with riffraff and tell me every detail. People with pending trials. People who'd been in jail. Cokeheads who'd pay for their next fix selling stolen videogames. Teenagers who'd shoplift whatever they could, wearing their baseball caps and baggy pants with cans of spray paint in their pockets. He'd sit next to them, picture this, wearing expensive suits and designer shoes. He liked to dress really well, even if he was just going out to steal a can of food. So young and talking about nineteenth-century writers. Philosophizing. Questioning everything. Theorizing about the group and the individual, about hypocrisy, about scapegoats, about God and destiny, and virginity, and sex. He used to say there wasn't a comparable pleasure to the pleasure of thinking. And no, he wasn't petulant or vain. He was just . . . exhaustive.

She briefly pauses. Her friend listens attentively with her lips slightly apart. In his corner, the boy seems more focused on his game than ever.

I know what you're asking yourself. How do I know that he was who he said he was? How did I know he was my age, for example? Why did I believe everything about him if I never actually saw him? But I really mean it: seeing him or not seeing him was irrelevant to me. A face, a body, what difference does it make? I had a hard time thinking of him as a real person anyway. He felt more like a character to me; even I acted like a character. I believed everything he said like you believe in a character, in a realm that's different than real life . . . I preferred it that way. Seeing him would've broken my fascination almost entirely. I don't expect you to get me . . .

The sound of a key in the door interrupts Sonia's monologue. She blinks, slightly startled, then composes herself and walks toward the door. *You made it. Hi, honey.*

Verdú takes off his backpack, kisses Sonia, and says hello to her friend. He picks up the boy and turns him almost completely upside down, laughing the whole time. The two women watch the show quietly.

I'm gonna go change out of this. I'll be right back, ladies, he says right before winking at them. *I want a drink too!*

Sonia looks at him walking away through the hallway. A stranger, she thinks. Lately that phrase comes to mind when she sees him walking from behind. His sloping shoulders; the curvature of his slightly hunched, broad back; his slow, almost ceremonious steps: *a stranger.* The boy trots happily behind him.

Once they're gone, Sonia continues.

There isn't much more to tell. I expected that the relationship would evolve, grow, but into what? He kept it going without asking anything of me. He just wanted my attention. It started to be excessive, even for me. I didn't have enough energy to reciprocate. I stopped feeling like it. He stopped surprising me and I got tired. I got married and I got tired. She lets out a sad laugh.

You miss him, huh?

The question floats between the two women for a few moments.

Sonia frowns and exclaims, *Miss?! You're not serious, are you? Of course I don't miss him!*

5. FOUR MONTHS LATER

I don't consider myself innocent. How could I?
The path of knowledge is the path of spiritual
corruption, it has been since the apple was bitten.
Thinking entails participating in that corruption.
Is a person more pure for not acting on their thoughts?
Anyone who thinks at least somewhat deeply
is vulnerable to remorse.

A CLICK OF the mouse. *Sending message.* She wrote it on impulse, before tending to anything else. In her new job, an "open work environment," people walk around in between desks. There isn't as much privacy as there was in the archive. The best way to get away with taking care of personal business is to do it very early or very late. She always takes some time to leave. It wouldn't look very good if she left as soon as the clock marked the end of the workday. She has responsibilities now. The work piles up on her desk: files, forms, printed emails. The documents aren't important. What counts is to have them there, piled up. A picture of her son smiling at the camera is the most she'll allow herself in front of her coworkers. She picks up the frame, looks carefully at the image. The photo was taken when the boy only had two bottom-front teeth. His lips are moist, his eyes joyfully scrunched. She was happy back then. She remembers it perfectly. They had spent a weekend at the beach. They sat the boy on the sand, right on the shore. Every time a wave reached him, calm, fresh, he reacted just as calmly, without fear. Everything was new at the time; but the feeling wore off. The novelty ended, that's all, she repeats to herself. She puts the picture down and cracks her knuckles. She goes back to her *Sent* folder, rereads the message she just sent.

I thought about you today. I should admit, I think about you often. I've wondered how you were this entire time, what you've been up to. I wondered if you thought about me, about us, about what happened to us. I have good memories. We weren't compatible, but we had luminous moments. I've written some short stories lately. I thought you'd be glad to know.

I'm exactly who I was before, he writes. *I haven't changed.* Sonia immediately has the same feeling she used to; it seems as though over three years without contact have happened in an afternoon. The only difference is that, since they lost touch, Knut has seen many women. Sonia's disappointed. What kind of women? she asks. He's met most of them online. Almost all of them are older than him: all kinds of women of all sorts of backgrounds. *Yes, I'm a great lover,* he says ironically. She thinks he's lost his innocence. Where did that profound, visceral rejection of sex go? Doesn't he find it cold to meet people like that? Knut expresses his surprise. Why would it be colder to start a relationship with someone you've met on the Internet than, say, after casually meeting at a peace demonstration? Aren't the randomness and the risk the same?

Nothing is said about what went on between them. Not a single reproach is offered by either. He confesses he's happy about the reunion. It's much better now that she has access to the Internet again. The letters had their charm but they took too long to arrive, he says; they would create distance between them. But, what's going on with her? Has she switched jobs? Is she still with Verdú? She's been writing, but what has she read lately? Would she send him some of her stories? He'd like nothing more than to read them.

Sonia says she has reservations about sharing her work with him. She knows he's a merciless judge. His opinion might determine the shape of the end product. Wouldn't she want to hear it precisely because of that? he replies. Doesn't she think that harsh criticism is what helps writers grow, learn the ropes? He'll send her more books if she sends him her writing. He's been keeping an excellent anthology of North American writers for months. He snagged it as soon as it came out, knowing that he'd have the opportunity to give it to her sooner or later. He grabbed two copies, one for each of them, so they could chat about the stories as they read them. He also has the complete short-story collections of Bellow, Nabokov, Faulkner, and Dinesen. He can send those too if she likes. He took them for her too. He acquired them as he would spot them during his normal excursions. *I hope it doesn't bother you,* he tells her. *I couldn't help thinking about you and trust that I'd be able to give them to you someday. It'll be a fair exchange, as well as a way to make up for all that's happened. It'll be both to our benefit and to that of literature.*

He kept stealing this whole time, then? Sonia asks.

Knut's very amused by the question. Most people think of stealing as transitory behavior, a phase teenagers go through, a mistake of those who haven't found their path in life. He's surprised to hear Sonia shares that perception. Why would he stop doing something he's done for so long? Only because he's aged a couple of years?

Stealing, he reflects, has more benefits than drawbacks.

Both direct benefits—in your case or the case of people who deserved gifts infinitely less than you—and indirect benefits—taking away from Isidoro and those like Isidoro helps spread altruism. It also doesn't hurt anyone. These are irrefutable facts, Knut says, however, they don't convince the average person. Theft always implies marginalization in the community. At this point, he's resorted to telling people that he steals because Greta Garbo used to do it; and then ask, do they consider themselves better than Greta Garbo? *Every now and then someone comes out with the if-Greta-Garbo-jumped-off-a-cliff cliché and I always say that Greta Garbo would've never jumped off a cliff. . . . She had better things to do—like steal, for example.*

How about shipments? Has he made similar gifts to other women? Has he told them about the exchange he shared with her? Knut admits he has, occasionally. It's mostly been DVDs, videogames and perfumes. He used to do it before and he'll continue for as long as he can. *Although not like with you . . .* He met a woman from another city to whom he also mailed books. Not as many as he sent Sonia, but quite a few. She would tell him which ones she felt like reading. He has to confess, she was very attractive, which kept him hooked for a long time. The allure wore off though. He simply lost the motivation to scour the stores of Cárdenas to find what she requested. Eventually they simply stopped. *It was all very different. I even lost money!* She never believed him. She thought he was a bookstore owner or a journalist and he was sending her promotional copies and making up the theft stories. *As though stealing was heroic*, he tells her. Knut thinks that she was testing him by asking for specific titles.

No, people don't usually understand him. Women understand him less than men. He had a debate with a French woman recently, a divorced professor, much older than them. They decided to meet directly at the hotel. It was fine, but he had trouble *doing it.* They had to stop midway and pick it up again later that night. The French woman insisted that it was okay. *"I know it's okay,"* he'd say to her, but his anxiety grew. She had paid for the hotel and he wanted to compensate her for the expense. So he proposed that she wait for him at a coffee shop while he grabbed her a couple of perfumes from the department store nearby, El Corte Inglés. She was very surprised. *"You look very normal. I wouldn't have expected you to do—that—for a living,"* she told him. *I don't know how she thought you're supposed to be dressed to steal. Success in stealing is achieved precisely by going unnoticed. But the group, which has created a prototype of the thief look, dictates its norms before there's time to reflect on them.* The French woman tried to convince him he was making a mistake. She said his arguments in favor of theft were fallacies. She thought stealing was wrong because injustices aren't made right with more injustices, because gifting something stolen makes the recipient an accomplice, because dignity isn't contained in material things . . . *that sort of reasoning,* Knut summarizes. He got tired of listening to her. Nonetheless, he considered her quite an intelligent woman. *If you had seen her . . . She had an elegance that I don't see in women here. She was an absolute lady. She wore Prada dresses and I could tell her lingerie had to be very expensive.* When he told her about Sonia and their exchange, she judged the relationship severely. *"Not acceptable"* she said. *Under any circumstance?* he insisted. *"No, not ever."* When she was young and couldn't afford books and records, she would've never accepted them if someone offered a similar arrangement. *Did someone ever offer?* Sonia asks him with disdain. *It's easy to form an opinion from the outside. Her argument is also inconsistent,* Knut says. *Morally speaking, compared to our barter, the average person engages in much more reprehensible behavior on any given day. Actually,* he adds, *I thought our old barter was a beautiful thing.*

Sonia feels the same way and tells him so.

She finally sends him the short stories to hear his verdict. Knut's response is the same for each one. He praises the whole but is viciously critical of the details. His analysis of every phrase, every word, is cruel. Most of the expressions she uses are imprecise, poorly written or simply redundant, they should've been omitted. He asks her to rewrite them based on his guidelines. His instructions are lengthier than the stories themselves. Sonia feels invaded by a discouraging feeling. She realizes this time it was she, on her own initiative, who got tangled in his demands again. She argues back. Why should everything be looked at through a magnifying glass? Perspective gets lost that way, it causes paralysis. But Knut is relentless. No, he says. One has to persevere, be constant, like in everything in life. That's the only way to bring out the best in oneself. When he runs out of arguments he asks her to do it as a favor: could she try it for his sake? Would it be so hard to please him? Even though rewriting them seems like a mountain of a chore, or a surgery, the result will be noticeable, he assures her. If only she'd let him help her. He'd comment on her work as she crafted it so she wouldn't lose motivation. She could, for example, write one page a day, send it to him, and work on the next one while he reviewed the first. Then she could return to the first page when he was reviewing the second. They'd make progress that way, two pages at a time. Would she be able to keep up with that rhythm? *You'd also benefit from reading Hemingway and Perutz. I'll go to the post office next week and send you a few of their books, along with the ones I had mentioned before. If you think of any other you'd like to have, tell me. You'll make me very happy if you accept them.*

She sends him a current picture. This time taken with a digital camera. She's sitting at the foot of a tree; it was taken during one of the hikes Verdú enjoys so much. The image quality is good. The photo reminds Sonia of her grandmother's picture, the one where she's sitting on a blanket: the same expression, the angle of the flexed legs, the hands interlaced over the knees, the wavy hair falling on the shoulders, messy. *This is what I look like now,* she tells Knut. He comments on what she's wearing. Knee-high workout leggings, wide T-shirt, thick socks, and hiking boots. *You don't dress like that all the time, do you? Tell me it's because you're in the great outdoors.* He analyzes the photo meticulously. *I pause on your smile and wonder what you were thinking. You seem distracted, withdrawn. I can't really make out the shape of your body. Excuse the question, but what bra size do you wear?*

Her breasts barely protrude in that outfit. He's heard that in addition to the numbers there's another measurement indicated by letters, A, B, C, which one is hers? Sonia is taken aback and flattered by his interest. She has no qualms in answering. It's 90B, why does he want to know? I'm just curious, Knut replies. The question about what size she wears, or any other private aspect of her life is nothing but a reflection of his undeniable enthusiasm for her, he explains. *I'm interested in everything about you. Now that I have you back I feel even more motivated to ask you.*

He also wants to know her shoe and clothing sizes, and in a few days he starts asking about more intimate details. Since his relationships are always sporadic, he tells her, he knows nothing about the minutiae of everyday life with someone. How is it to sleep with the same person every night? How often do you *do it*? Is there a progression in your practices or is it mere repetition of your beginnings? Like in previous years, he avoids using words he considers too strong. *I admit I am a prude*, he says, *but when it comes to sex I prefer repression, and the perversion that comes with it.*

However, once the language is sanitized, he seems to have no issue sharing specifics about his escapades. He doesn't brag or embellish. He offers antiseptic descriptions without hiding his detachment or omitting any sordid portion. *Always that sadness at the end*, he says, *a vague longing or a sort of image. Occasionally, after I've satisfied the first impulse, I imagine your face—or to be more exact, your face getting closer to mine—and I think that's how I should always picture you: next to me, looking at me.* Sometimes he has impotence issues. *I have to warm up*, he explains. *When I am going to meet up with someone, I masturbate before, but without com . . . I do that a few times so I can show up when my tension is fully built up.* This was the strategy he used with a woman he had been seeing in the last few weeks. She lived alone and was about fifty. She was the head of a department in a bank, no children. He visited her in her luxury duplex in an expensive

street in Cárdenas. They'd meet about two or three times a week
and have pizza and ice cream and watch TV after *doing it*. Knut
felt comfortable in that house, she never asked about his life,
they didn't even have to speak at all if they didn't feel like it. But
one day as he was leaving, she leaned softly on the front-door
frame and announced that they wouldn't be seeing each other
anymore. *I realized right there that I was going to miss the pizza
and the ice cream more than the fu . . .* he confesses.

Sonia asks him how someone with a moral worldview like his
could be so indifferent all of a sudden. Isn't his apathetic attitude
toward sex almost cruel? But Knut doesn't see a contradiction in
his stance. *What I'd like to be able to do is pass on sex completely,*
he says. *The sexual impulse always ends up taking on a social layer
I detest; it's made up of moral conjectures, bourgeois pretensions,
and the clear absence of more intellectual ambitions. I aspire to
keep it at the level of impulse, without imbuing it with anything
else. Is that cruelty?* The soul, spirituality, or whatever you agree
to call it, should stay outside of sex, untouched by it. *I despise
that destructive vocabulary some men use to talk about women, as
if they had just been at war and, in the name of patriotism, they
were bragging about seizing and killing the enemy; but I also hate
that false view of sex as something playful, a game that's akin to
pastimes of our era, like rafting or bridge bungee.* Sex is torment,
pain, and loneliness, an animal vestige we can't escape. *Plus,
regardless of how many disguises we put on it, sex is just . . . sex.*

They agree that Sonia should pick up the package directly at the
post office. This way she can avoid both Verdú and her coworkers seeing it. Knut warns her that this time the box is bigger and
heavier than normal. *Realize it has books I picked out for you years
ago. The merchandise has accumulated.*

Sonia arrives in a rush. She doesn't dare double-park, the
idea of another driver honking at her is intolerable. She looks
at the clock on the dashboard every now and then while she

drives through the surrounding streets she goes around a few times before finding a spot. Once there, she has to stand in line for a long while. The woman in front of her is taking her time giving instructions for a money order. Sonia watches how she leans on the counter, she stares at her bulky body and her long, dull, shapeless hairdo. A money order? she now thinks, impatient. She doesn't understand what the point of a money order is anymore. Isn't it a million times faster to make a payment online? If the woman isn't finished soon, she'll need to call her son's daycare center to let them know she'll be late. She watches the woman's weight shift from one leg to the other as she stands scratching the back of her neck, indecisive. *Why is there only one line?* an elderly man complains behind Sonia. *Sir, we are the only post office open past five*, one of the employees says from behind her section of the counter. The money-order woman takes out her wallet, pays, signs, and finally leaves followed by the echo of her high heels hitting the floor. Sonia approaches the counter and shows her ID. The clerk prints a code, heads toward the back of the room, and stands still for a moment. After a few seconds of looking around the packages she hesitates again. Sonia speaks to her from afar. It should be a bigger package than those, she says. The clerk doesn't show signs of listening. She disappears through a narrow door in the very back and comes out with another employee who has a different kind of uniform, maybe the manager. They talk in a low voice, give Sonia a long look, and move around some boxes and envelopes. Is there any way they could know what she's receiving is stolen? Sonia thinks instantly. Is *that* what's happening? Are they going to call someone? The police? She feels a strong pressure in her chest and her hands start shaking. They keep shifting packages around, inspecting addresses. Every now and then they turn around to look at her. The elderly man complains again, *Why aren't there more clerks out here?* he groans. His chin trembles, he taps his cane against the laminate floor. Sonia turns around and notices the blue hue of the skin on his fists, marked with veins and brown spots. Like quail eggs, she thinks. When she turns back, the clerk is approaching her, wobbling from the weight of the box between her arms. She places it on the counter with effort and reads the labels written in all caps with an ambiguous expression, her eyes follow the precise, childlike handwriting. Sonia signs the receipt and tries to lift the box. It's too heavy, the corners hurt her wrists. She struggles to walk toward the door. It's starting to rain again. She regrets parking so far away. She won't be able to carry the package all the way there by herself. She puts it on the floor, and looks at the time on her phone. A large man with a mustache is smoking near the post office entrance. She asks him if he can watch the package while she brings her car. *Sure girl*, he says and looks at her from top to bottom with a half-smile. He helps her put the box in the trunk when she comes back. *What's in there, girl? A dead body or two?* he laughs. His teeth are big, his lips are thin and have a burgundy tone. Sonia laughs as well and thanks him. Her hair is wet from the rain, she feels it sticking to her cheeks. She gets in the car and steps on the gas leaving as fast as possible. It's late, very late, but she stops a couple of blocks ahead—this time she double-parks—comes out, and opens the trunk in the rain which is now soaking her clothes and shoes.

The packaging is tight as usual. It can't be opened without a knife or scissors, but Sonia uses her fingernails anyway, she rips the tape from one edge and struggles to pull the cardboard flap until she tears a large enough hole. She can see books, many books packed with sheets of newspaper in between for protection. There's something else. Before confirming what it is, Sonia already knows. She touches it for a few seconds before taking it out. Just her size, B cup, soft to the touch, with underwire, black with blood-red accents. It's a Calvin Klein. The price tag is still on, 55 euro. She throws it back in hurriedly, without putting it in its fabric bag. She gets back in the car. Her phone is ringing but she doesn't hear it. She starts the engine, smiling.

It fits perfectly, she says. Really? Calvin Klein uses American sizes, so he initially hesitated: 90B, he explains, is 34B for them. Knut didn't always know this. The equivalencies weren't specified in the paper tag. He did see it later in the smaller tag inside the bra. He had to make a few rounds before grabbing it, even though it didn't have a *security tag*—those plastic clips equipped with a dye that stains the item of clothing if someone bold decides to break it. It must have belonged to a new batch that hadn't been tagged yet. If she looks closely, all the lingerie at El Corte Inglés has a *tag;* from the Dim to the Jennifer Lopez and the Calvin Klein to the Simone Pérèle. All of it except for the lingerie from La Perla, they use plastic stickers for that collection, which are much more discreet.

Does Sonia know that brand? It's Italian, incredibly sophisticated, very expensive. Maybe the company thinks security tags take away from the beauty of the pieces and refuses to follow the department store policy. It was founded by a woman named Ada Masotti in Bologna in the nineteen-fifties. She named the company after pearls because they used to transport the lingerie in velvet-lined cases, like the ones used by jewelers. *Remarkable finesse, don't you think?* Knut comments. *Masotti probably did more for women's lib than many feminists.*

The Calvin Klein she got was easy to take. He simply made sure that the salesclerks were busy and the cameras weren't looking. *A matter of patience, as usual.* When the right moment presented itself he swiftly walked through the section and tossed it in a bag without stopping. He headed for the perfume section at the same speed and used the escalator to go downstairs. None of the camera lenses moved. A security guard was yawning by the exit through which he left; and another, wearing the same red uniform, was chewing gum, looking resigned. *Very easy, you see? And I didn't even bring a jacket to hide it in . . .*

Does it really fit well? Does it accentuate her breasts? The tag said that the model, "Naked Glamour," has a push-up effect. Does it really do that?

He thought so much about her on the escalator, when he was carrying it in the bag . . . He thought about her so intensely. He remembered what she's said about the dog her neighbors keep locked up in the patio and pictured Sonia looking at the dog sadly. He also remembered what she told him years ago, when she let that teacher film her. He pictured her rewriting her stories, struggling to stay awake at home next to her son, whom she just put to bed. Those for instance, and the many other details of her life only he knows about, are enough reason for Sonia to deserve that bra, and all the books, and all the gifts in the world that he can give her. *Really, I left the store elated, completely overjoyed. For you. Thanks to you.*

Have you ever thought of giving everything up to write? he asks one day. She already knows his opinion about family life. Family and writing are incompatible; this actually isn't an opinion, it's an objective fact. She should live alone, and dedicate her time—her freedom—to reading and writing. She shouldn't work either. Unless she lets go of all those imposed bougie aspirations, her results will always be mediocre, or way beneath her talent. Sonia thinks he's joking at the beginning. How would that even be possible? Is he out of his mind? How would she make a living? And her child? How can he think she would give him up? Plus—she adds proudly—she doesn't want to separate from her husband. She doesn't see the need to be so drastic. Are there no writers who have families? Didn't Kafka, like so many others, have an office job? Not that she's comparing herself to Kafka, but just as there are examples for one scenario, there are for its opposite. Knut assures her he's being completely serious. He feels irritated that she would take it so lightly. *I realize the idea seems strange to you, but you'll see little by little that it isn't as difficult as you think. In fact, it's very easy, you only have to want it. But you are too lazy and you only let your bougie aspirations guide you.* She's the drastic one: living alone doesn't have to imply not seeing her son or Verdú. Why couldn't she visit them often in this scenario? In reality she, who brags about being a modern, independent woman, never stops to think of things from a different angle. *I bet that to you notions like "mothers should be the main caretakers of children" and "the most important thing in life are friends" are as irrefutable as facts like horses eat alfalfa or the Volga flows into the Caspian sea. It's interesting too how the language you use betrays you. How you always give a tinge of righteous victimhood to your retorts. You say "my child," instead of my son, or "my husband" instead of Verdú.*

What Sonia thought was funny in the beginning is starting to bother her. What hurts the most, she tells him, is that he labels her as being lazy and having bougie aspirations. What does he really know about her? Does he know that she gets up early to make breakfast for her son, bathe him, get him dressed, drive him to daycare, go to work, make dinner, and take care of him until her husband, or Verdú, or however he prefers that she call him, gets home? That she then goes to visit her mom and helps her with her grandmother and her sibling? That it's after all those things that she reads and tries to write something that meets his expectations? *Now you're going to say that I am using a victim tone, but I am really offended by the image you have of me.*

You say I have bougie aspirations . . . but it's you who made fun of me for eating kebabs, who goes nuts eating at high-end restaurants, who knows all about clothing brands and brags about not having to work a job to earn a living.

Knut insists that she shouldn't feel upset or insulted: he's merely describing the situation impartially. Are work and family not the pillars of the bourgeois system? Why is she so afraid to step outside and look at the structure? When he poses those kinds of questions, he's not trying to provoke her, he's trying to help her. *But you're too used to flattery. You tell me I'm crazy and that I exaggerate, yet when I describe my feelings for you while going down the escalator, you don't think I'm crazy or exaggerated. You limit yourself to acting coy, although you obviously love to hear about it. You should be just as flattered when I point out your mistakes, because what motivates me in both cases is exactly the same: the immense love I feel for you.*

Escaping the bourgeois system is first achieved by shifting the property paradigm. To whom do goods belong? Who has the right to own them or to claim ownership? When Knut tells her about his theft experiences, she pretends to be curious or shows a degree of disbelief. She says she approves of the practice—or doesn't say anything—but he's aware that what he's relating is completely foreign to her. Would she ever venture to steal something just to try it? Theft opens the mind like no other experience. As much as Sonia claims to understand his principles, the only way to know if she's actually convinced by them is if she tries it, at least once. This would also be the most direct path for them to become closer. Does she want to know how any given afternoon is for him? She should go to El Corte Inglés and steal some books, then tell him how she felt. Only then can they truly have a discussion about bougie behavior, work, and freedom.

Sonia doesn't do it at El Corte Inglés, she tries it at a bookstore, La Casa del Libro. She doesn't plan it. She simply happens to walk by the bookstore while she's out shopping for clothes for her son and remembers Knut's words. She feels the impulse to try it and goes in the shop. First she picks up some books and feels gently for a security tag under the barcode sticker. It's there. She located a camera at the furthest corner of the store when she walked in, but now she's too panicked to look at it. She feels like she has guilt written all over her face before even committing the act. Should she try deactivating the security tag? Knut's explained to her how it's done but she can't fathom doing it right now. She'll have to take one that's *clean*. She pushes the stroller to the foreign literature section and pretends to browse for a while. She picks out two books, Tobias Wolff, Peter Stamm. Knut has spoken highly of both. Does she have an interest in them? She doesn't even read the back covers. She slides her finger over the barcode stickers. They're flat. What if they have magnetic alarm stickers inside the pages? They most likely don't but she flips through some pages, just in case. Knut's explained that each establishment has its own system, and it's usually only one kind of security tag. *They're books, not jewels*, he said. The boy starts kicking impatiently, strapped to his chair. *We're almost done, honey.* She crouches briefly and tosses the Tobias Wolff book in the bag hanging from the back of the stroller. When she gets back up she sees a fat man near her who's sweating. He's wearing a wrinkled shirt and a belt that's tighter than necessary. The man mumbles something under his breath, he sounds annoyed. An undercover security guard? She dismisses the idea right away. There's no way they have an undercover guard in a bookstore. Especially one who looks like that. He walks toward her and looks her straight in the eye. She smiles nervously and apologizes, moving the stroller out of the way. She puts the other book on the shelf and rushes out of the aisle. What would happen if the alarm goes off? She can always say she was distracted and forgot she put the book there. Shopping with the child makes that the perfect excuse: *Oh! I tossed it there and completely forgot.* Knut is right, the more *normal* your appearance, the more well-adjusted you seem, the easier it is to go unnoticed. She tries to calm down. She stops near the entrance to show the boy a box of colored pencils. *Like the ones you have at home*, she says. They leave the store. Her heart is beating frenetically; she feels her cheeks flush immediately but nothing happens. No sound goes off. She

walks faster, looks around. She continues to walk along with
the crowd exiting the mall. Evening comes.

Only after making it home does she work up the courage
to take the book out of the bag. With a glass of wine in one
hand, she looks at it, satisfied. After the glass is empty she pours
herself a refill, victorious. She would write Knut immediately
to tell him about it but she doesn't want him to know she has
Internet at home. She texts him. *I snagged a book. It's by Tobias
Wolff. I'll tell you about it tomorrow.* Knut replies immediately. *I
am proud of you. I can't wait to hear more!*

What seems strange to him is that she took a book he's already
given her. *When you told me it was by Wolff, I obviously thought of
a different title.* Sonia feels embarrassed. She apologizes. He must
forgive her, that bad memory of hers tricked her again. Now
she realizes why the cover seemed so familiar, but she's sure he'll
understand . . . He's sent so many books! She hasn't read quite
a few of them yet, to which the ones in his latest package—full
to the brim—are now added. She thinks there may even be a
genetic cause behind her problem. Her mom is also forgetful,
and her grandmother, well, she'd rather not discuss what state
her mind is in. *But you went to college,* he says. *You had to have
memorized something to pass exams, right?* Yes, but she'd forget
it right after. He has to believe her, as much as she tries not to,
she just forgets things. *Okay, well we've talked about memory
a thousand times already,* Knut replies. *My extensive advice has
evidently been pointless.* It isn't an isolated incident as far as he's
concerned. It's another piece of evidence of Sonia's fickleness.
She may think that beyond the inconveniences it causes it isn't
very serious, but it is.

That afternoon, he tells her, he had a conversation with the
girl from the dry cleaner's for a similar reason. He'd brought in
a pair of pants with ice-cream stains. He remembered it had
at least four: two large and two small. Although once dry they

weren't obvious. The girl circled two of them with her chalk and gave him his ticket just like that. What about the other stains? he asked. Wouldn't she circle them too? No. It wasn't necessary, she added. They'd remove them just the same. Then why circle some stains and not others? The girl just said with a smile that they'd take care of all of it for him and it would look perfect. *But my concern was a legitimate one. Wasn't it? After almost an hour discussing it, the girl didn't shift her stance by a millimeter. She didn't even accept my help in finding the stains that she hadn't circled.*

That night he could hardly sleep. In addition to the incident at the dry cleaner's—which had already raised his stress levels— he tried to find the balance between two simultaneous realities. On the one hand, the fact that Sonia had gone out to steal, the text she sent him after, the joy she immediately wanted to share; on the other, the mistake, the forgetfulness, the basic lack of interest she demonstrated. He pictured them as separate, unbridgeable dimensions. Later that night, he was woken up by a bursting sound, like a light bulb cracking. He thought one from the ceiling lamp must have burnt out and tried to fall back asleep. The second burst came shortly after. He then realized nothing had burnt out. Did his imagination produce two bursting sounds? It's very possible. The most accurate explanation is that they were a product of his nerves. That's what he goes through when something is bothering him. *All that because of your forgetfulness. Can you really not see how terrible it can be?*

Sonia looks out the window over the kitchen sink. The dog is sleeping in a corner of the patio next to a dry rack covered with carelessly placed bedsheets. She watches it while she drinks a beer. The animal's torso slowly expands and contracts. It's a hot day, there aren't any shaded areas it can sleep under. Still, it seems content. The last time she mentioned the dog to Knut, he questioned her concern. Was she being sincere? he asked. Given the opportunity, would she do something about it? Would she explain to her neighbors the reasons why she thinks it shouldn't be kept there day after day? If they didn't listen, would she be willing to report the abuse? *Based on your personality, even the way you act with me, I've noticed that you always avoid conflict. That's why you opt for silence when you don't like something.*

Sonia closes the kitchen window and opens another beer. She leans against the counter feeling somewhat dizzy, her attention is diluted, fuzzy. She thinks about Knut. She takes a sip of beer, closes her eyes; she thinks about Knut. She got a new package from him at work that morning. It was a much smaller and much lighter box. For the first time, it didn't contain books, just three lingerie sets from La Perla and two perfumes. All still with the tag in place. She held the pieces between her fingers in disbelief. She even risked her coworkers seeing it. He was right. That brand was extremely expensive. She recognizes the sophistication in the details: lace, sheer fabrics, different textures—satin, silk. Yes, everything is elegant and refined but still, she asks herself, how can a bra cost 180 euro? And underwear 120? A 300-euro set, and the box came with three, plus the two perfumes—also designer brands, also expensive. She thanked him with fervor instantly via email. He replied almost immediately as well. Really? Was she happy? Did she think they'd fit? Would she tell him all about it the next day? Could she text him an update in the meantime? *Ohhh my favorite is the mint-green one with the lace flower pattern, the one that's sheer right around . . . I hope it fits because it's a sublime piece, very arousing.*

As much as it surprises her, lingerie is not difficult to *obtain*. He's mentioned to her before that La Perla doesn't use those horrendous white security tags with the dye but very discreet plastic tags inside. All one has to do is place stickers over them to deactivate the alarm and voilà. What he did first was take the garments to an area without cameras. He knows the stores really well, so it just takes some strategizing on his part. The only difficult part was making sure the tops matched the bottoms. The pale pink bra, for example, he actually got at a different mall, six subway stops away from the first. *It would've made no difference if it were twenty stops,* he tells her. *Once I start, there's no stopping me.*

Sonia chugs her beer and hesitates before opening the next one. Verdú will notice, she thinks, but she gets it out of the fridge and promises herself she'll replace them before he comes back. She hears the sound of the TV in the other room, her son laughing in front of the screen. She continues her train of thought, hazy, confused. She tells herself the pleasure of receiving gifts, of feeling like Knut's object of devotion, is blinding her. He's constructing an image of her and she's allowing it. She'll end up hurting him. How can she prevent it though? She's never asked him for anything, she broods. She voices it somewhat out loud, for herself, as if she were defending her case in a trial in which both were the defendants. *No, I never asked him for anything.*

She tosses the beer bottles in a garbage bag and takes her keys and wallet.

Sweetheart, I'm going downstairs to the store. Do me a favor and don't move an inch from here. OK? I'll be right back.

The boy, fascinated by cartoons, doesn't turn around. She comes over to hug him from behind. When she goes to kneel, she stumbles on her own foot and falls. She struggles to get up. She sprained her ankle. She rubs it to ease the pain.

Did you hear me? she repeats. *Mommy's gonna be right back.*

After taking a shower, while her son is sleeping and Verdú is making dinner, she tries on the lingerie as quickly as possible, locked in the bathroom. The quality of the fabrics, soft and delicate, is extraordinary. Even so, she prefers cotton. Of the three bras, two are too small and one actually chafes her skin. The underwear isn't flattering either: she finds the erotic pretensions of the pieces ridiculous when used to dress imperfect bodies. Too much flesh sticking out over here, too uncomfortable there. Plus, Verdú could care less about that sort of thing.

Gonna be a while?

Almost done, she answers. She hurries to shove all the lingerie back in a bag that she hides under a stack of clean towels. *Coming!* she says; but she takes a moment to text Knut. *Everything's perfect. Amazing. I'm so, so happy.*

The next morning, however, she inserts her concerns in the conversation. Isn't he putting himself too much at risk? she asks. Wasn't taking these pieces too bold? It's not the same to take a 40-euro perfume as a 200-euro bra. She of course likes it, she feels flattered to be the recipient of his effort, but she won't wear the pieces often enough to justify that kind of exposure. He shouldn't send more perfumes. She already has too many. She's nowhere near running out. But those arguments don't convince Knut. He tells her to wear perfume more often. *You can even wear it to be at home, to cook, why not? That will set you apart from other women.* About the risk, it isn't something he needs to minimize: he's aware of it and he's absolutely willing to assume it. Knut thrives when challenged. His desire to please her, to make her happy, grows with the difficulty of that challenge. *Believe it or not, hunting for the perfect piece for you gives me joy beyond words.* Actually, he admits, those have been the happiest days in the last few years of his life. *I swear I'm not exaggerating.*

If you lived in Cárdenas, we'd meet this afternoon and I'd show you. We'd go to two or three malls, and I'd snag anything you like . . . There's so much to pick from. To end the afternoon I'd grab a few videogames so you could sell them at a secondhand store and we would dine like kings in a good hotel restaurant. I'd ask you for a long kiss before we said goodbye. You could leave to go on a date with a lover, wearing something I gave you. That's all it would take to make me happy. We'd both be happy.

6. TRANSACTION

No, she responds, she didn't keep the original box. She mentioned it in the ad: <<*Does not include original box.*>> They'll be shipped in a box, of course, individually wrapped for protection, just not the original box. The merchandise is original. She guarantees it one hundred percent. She encourages her to read the reviews from past customers. Everyone has been happy with their purchase and given her profile a five-star rating.

The buyer seems reluctant, but does complete the transaction. She requests rush shipping. She's planning to wear them at a wedding, she adds. No problem, Sonia replies. She'll ship them as soon as she receives the payment confirmation. The transaction confirmation is in her inbox a few minutes later. Sonia looks inside Verdú's side of the closet, almost empty by now. She doesn't see anything she can use. She climbs on a chair to look in the top shelf and finds a shoebox in good shape. She takes it to the dining room.

Where are you keeping the tissue paper we got for school?

The boy stops playing, tilts his head, and looks up trying to remember. He thinks for a moment with a chipped Transformer in his hand. *Mm . . . I don't know.*

Come on, remember: where did you put it?

I don't know.

Sonia huffs. She crumples some sheets of newspaper to make a nest inside the box. Fuck it, she tells herself. What matters is the merchandise. She stops to look at the shoes one last time before wrapping them. Black, velvet high-heels—about three and a half inches—with a silver metallic tip. She checks the soles. She sees some black marks from trying them on and scratches some of them off with her nails. She straightens the tag with her fingers. *Satin pump with asymmetric vamp: solid color, leather sole, narrow toe line, covered heel. Made in Italy. 295 euro.* She places them on the crumpled paper, closes the box, and tapes it up. She dials a number on her phone.

Hey, I need to be there a bit later. I have to stop by the post office.

She closes her eyes as she listens to the voice on the other side.

OK, OK. Look, it's fine. I can stop by your place first and we'll figure out the situation with gramma; but I need you to watch him while I go to the post office then. It'll be quicker if I go by myself.

Another silence. She taps impatiently on the shoebox.

Yes, mom: it—is—necessary that I go today. It's urgent. It can't wait 'til tomorrow. I'll explain later.

She hangs up and calls her son. *Get ready. Your room can stay like that. We need to go now.*

Are we going to dad's?

No. You'll see dad next weekend.

The boy runs down the hallway and comes back holding his shoes. Sonia helps him tie his shoelaces.

Perfect. Come on. We gotta run.

She looks at the clock. Seven o'clock. The post office closes at eight. She writes the shipping address on a piece of paper. She holds the boy's hand and carries the shoebox under her other arm, leaning it against her hip.

Let's go!

7. A YEAR BEFORE

*My behavior isn't irrational. What may be
is how easily I adopt it,
how I succumb to it again and again. But
violence—and my behavior is violence
in its purest state—originates in the
reptilian brain we all have left over,
a feature which no evolutionary stage
has managed to eliminate.*

I GOT EIGHT more La Perla sets.

Eight? Sonia isn't surprised anymore, she just goes along with Knut's latest self-imposed challenge. He writes enthusiastic descriptions of the pieces before shipping them. *You'll find all kinds and colors,* he says: white, beige, purple, coral, baby blue, black, pieces with printed patterns, silk-thread lace, synthetic-fiber lace . . . *I think the black one is particularly wonderful.* The minutely detailed account follows. *It's from the brand's exclusive collection. Just the bra, which is double layered, is 243 euro. Seriously, when you hold it in your hands and take a look at it, you just know it's very well made, whether you're interested or not in the world of lingerie.* Eight sets, Sonia repeats. She doesn't know what she'll do with so much underwear. *Well, wear it, right?* Knut replies. *I'm sure it fits beautifully.* She's still resistant. No, she won't be able to wear it just like that. Verdú isn't going to simply believe she spent all this money on lingerie out of the blue—it's spare money they're far from having . . . *Tell him the truth, then,* he suggests. *Tell him a friend gave it to you.* Is he nuts? Sonia laughs in writing. He can't be serious. Of course he's serious, Knut replies. Why would Verdú feel jealous? Would he actually have a reason to be? Knut has no intention of taking anything away from him. Their spheres of action are entirely different. It's easy to be confused by the lingerie if the situation is viewed from outside their relationship, but one mustn't give in to the first thought that comes to mind. Knut doesn't infringe on Verdú's territory because he enjoys the pieces much more and before Verdú would, from the moment he starts hunting for them. He likes coveting them, concealing them under his own clothes, kissing them when he gets home, picturing how they look on her body, describing them to her. That imaginary construct, "what is yet to be" he says, is where the allure of sex comes from. *I am perfectly fine with forgoing the next step. You know I don't aspire to f . . . you. Do you think that's my intention? It isn't. I'm satisfied with playing a small part in your life.*

That said, does she have any qualms with taking the pieces? *Of course I'll take them,* Sonia assures him. She just wants him to be aware that she will have to hide them. She'll never, or almost never, be able to wear them. Is it still worth it to give them to her? He insists: she doesn't have to wear them if she can't find the time. She can simply keep the lingerie in a box. *Just like I enjoy putting the box together before shipping it, you can enjoy opening your box, caressing the pieces, calmly trying them on, and putting them back inside. To me, just that is incredibly provocative.*

In all honesty, he wishes he could've gotten many more things for her. He blames himself for his recent poor performance. He wanted to *acquire* a pair of silk-satin culottes but it was impossible. The salesclerk wouldn't take her eyes off him, yet he also wasn't skilled enough to skirt her surveillance. They almost caught him putting a sticker on a corset at another mall, and he was too slow to find her size at a third store, missing the chance to seize upon a larger booty. He's not sleeping well lately, his arms tingle when he's in bed, and his calves become stiff with any slight change in posture. When he finally falls asleep, he does so full of muscle tension, and he wakes up with neck and back pain. He has constant nightmares.

He's been dreaming a lot about his childhood, mostly about being in his mom's hometown. The images in his dreams, he tells her, have the texture of Victor Sjöström's initial nightmare in *Wild Strawberries*. He's told her repeatedly he doesn't care too much for film because, as an art form, it's too dependent on social and financial factors. Film is a group production, while literature is the spiritual fruit of none other than the individual confronting himself on his own. Nevertheless, he's seen the great films of the last century. Naturally, all or almost all of Bergman's work. And he's not telling her this to brag; only because, curiously, in his last dream there was also a clock: the fact that time had stopped was central in making it a nightmare. The town was black and white and felt almost deserted although people were there. He couldn't see them, but everyone who was usually around when he went as a child was there: his cousins, the children that would always harass him the first few days but would later get used to him and leave him alone, the old ladies in mourning dressed in black sitting on their front porches. The fruit and bread trucks arrived at the main square. He saw people walking in that direction ready to go shopping for the day, and he decided to join them, yet walked at a distance. The clock in the town square said it was 9:10 but according to his watch, the time was 9:17. This caused him infinite despair. *Those seven minutes existed in the realm of impossibility.*

After this kind of dream he usually wakes up soaked in sweat and has palpitations that can last for hours. *All this affects my performance when filling up the coffers.* Could it be a consequence and not the cause? Sonia asks. *It must stress you very much to take such expensive merchandise.* He denies it. *Look, if anything stresses me out, it's thinking that one of the pieces may get damaged, however slightly, in the process. The mere possibility of it happening while I take them, or during the shipping, fills me with enormous grief. I imagine this form of fetishism is rooted in my childhood.*

As a boy, he used to suck on his ring and middle fingers to go to sleep, while rhythmically rubbing his upper lip with his index finger. He got used to using a soft handkerchief or any piece of worn cloth to do this, the thinner the better. His mom would set aside old handkerchiefs for him and he would carefully fold them to keep under his pillow. He secretly used her underwear too. *Back then she would spend the entire day at the casino without bothering to take care of me,* he tells Sonia. *Now she's hooked on TV psychics and doesn't speak a word to me, but I couldn't care less at this point.* He'd take her garments to rub against his face and smell them. *It had a calming effect on me; all of a sudden the universe was in order, one which I could live in placidly.* One time, when he was ten or eleven, his mother found out he had hidden a nightgown of hers that she thought she'd lost. When faced with the boy's stubborn silence in response to the question of why he hid it, she lost her patience. She shook and slapped him several times in the trance of rage. Knut bit his cheeks to hold back the tears. He doesn't consider it a bad memory though. It was the logical consequence of his behavior, he says; even at that age he was able to understand that and accept it.

El Corte Inglés doesn't carry La Perla in Sonia's city. She browses around the lingerie section a couple of times, looking at the sets from other brands. Some are so light they come off the hanger at the slightest touch. She notices the kinds of pieces she'd never paid attention to before: bralettes, garters, lace bras, minuscule thongs. All of them have clips. She sees two cameras, very few customers, and a store clerk constantly checking the sections with the highest prices, ready to make a sale. Sonia wonders how Knut is able to steal in these conditions. His claims aside, Cárdenas can't be that different. She takes her son's hand, they head to the supermarket section.

She tosses a bag of apples, a package of chicken breasts, and an egg carton in her shopping basket. On the way to the registers, she stops in front of the cosmetics display. It has cheap brands, plenty of items don't have any packaging or obvious security devices. Knut's told her that when she wants something she should take it without hesitation. *The worst thing you can do is browse by the same spot multiple times. Just act confidently, decide what you like, and put it in your bag immediately.* Sonia picks a small makeup bottle. Maybelline Superstay 24 H, tone 4, medium coverage, 10.90 euro. She's never worn that kind of makeup; she's always thought it looks artificial on people's skin; but she can try it out. The bottle is small, it barely weighs anything. She closes her fist, puts her hand in the shopping basket and starts talking loudly to her son. On the next aisle she crouches near the bleach and ammonia in the bottom shelf and drops the makeup bottle in her purse. She looks at merchandise in two or three more aisles, then heads toward the registers and gets in a line. She feels surprisingly calm. Victorious. Satisfied. The boy talks the entire time, she entertains his chitchat. The rhythmic sound of the scanners detecting labels paces the interaction. When her turn is up she asks for a bag and puts the fruit, the chicken, and the eggs inside. She takes out her wallet to pay and steps near the register's security antenna. An unexpected beep violently hits her eardrums, and the red light at the top of the antenna flashes intermittently. The noise is piercing. The color, accusatory. The cashier looks at her sternly, she raises one eyebrow. Her son is also looking at her, amazed. She stutters, incapable of forming a single word. *Like if it were happening to someone else*, she'll tell Knut later.

Scan your purse again ma'am, says the cashier. Sonia puts it near the antenna. The unmistakable beep goes off again. Sonia opens her mouth slightly and gives the cashier an embarrassed look.

Do you have an item in your purse you haven't purchased ma'am?

Sonia notices the security guard walking toward her on her left-hand side. The navy-blue hue of his uniform, the crackling of the walkie-talkie. The cashier signals for him to wait, to hold on. *The customer will take it out on her own.* Sonia opens her purse and hands her the makeup bottle. She explains herself babbling, short of breath.

I can't believe I didn't notice I put it there. We were in a hurry . . . I get so distracted when I'm out with my boy.

The cashier doesn't return the smile. She scans the bottle and points at the price on the screen.

Will you be purchasing it or should we just put it back?

No, I'll pay for it, of course. I was going to pay for it.

The skin on her ears is burning. The boy is now clinging to her leg, completely quiet. Sonia pays, takes her son's hand, and almost drags him to the exit door. When they walk by the security guard, she looks down and overhears what the cashier says to him.

That was quite a show . . . Normal-looking people, huh? What do you know?

Sonia gets in her car. She sees her son's reflection in the rearview mirror. He's sitting almost motionless in his car seat, stunned. She hears the squealing tires of other cars rubbing against the parking-lot pavement. Their headlights illuminate her hands, shaking on top of the steering wheel. It takes her a few minutes to start the car.

She shouldn't think too much of it, Knut tells her the next day. There were no consequences, so she has nothing to worry about.

The cashier was discreet. She didn't shame her in public—probably because of the boy. Will she give up over that? She's already snagged a few books. Why not continue with books then? *I'm really not good at this,* Sonia says. She admits she felt paralyzed when it happened. She should be more persevering, Knut insists, but he doesn't want to pressure her. He can provide anything she needs. She shouldn't stop asking him for anything.

That same morning she had gotten the package with the eight La Perla sets, plus some perfume bottles, a Sensilis lotion, the complete short stories of Katherine Mansfield, and something unexpected: a pair of shoes. Armani. Deep blue. Extremely high heels with ankle straps, 229 euro.

You shouldn't send me this, she says. *I'm not sure I deserve it. You're risking your neck for something I'll never be able to wear.* Why? Knut replies. Does she not like them? Yes, of course she likes them. She simply can't think of a time she would ever wear them. She usually wears sandals, flats, and boots. Wearing three-inch heels doesn't fit her lifestyle. *Well, keep them for when it does. There will surely be a time when you'll need them. Even if you just wear them once, or only try them on when you're home alone, that's enough for me.*

Sonia throws the lingerie on the bed and starts trying each set on in front of the mirror, wearing the Armani shoes. She looks grotesque at first. She turns off the lights and leaves on only the softer bedside reading lamp. She lets down her hair and shakes it. Now, in the darkness of the room, she feels the effect of the transformation. Lioness, she thinks. Knut likes to use that word to describe her. *I picture you this way often, like a lioness. I can just see you in my mind. I see the promise of sex. I get really turned on picturing your loose long hair and your body wrapped in the pieces I got for you.*

She picks up her cellphone and takes pictures in front of the mirror. She later puts her home clothes back on and bunches the lingerie up inside the box. She sits on the bed and thumbs through the pictures she just took. She first deletes the ones she doesn't like. She looks closely at the flattering ones. Zooms in. Deletes a few more. She finally settles on two. In one she's wearing the black set that entices Knut so much. In the other, a white set with a garter. Her legs are slightly open and her head is leaning forward in both pictures. Her face is blocked by her forearm as she holds the cellphone to snap the picture. She hardly recognizes herself. She thumbs through both images for a few minutes. After a while, she deletes them too.

Everything rushes forward after that moment: the fantasy awakens her curiosity and her curiosity feeds the fantasy. She realizes none of it makes sense unless he can see her. Shouldn't she give him some kind of reward? Is it enough to just extend her hands to receive? She overcomes her lack of motivation to write to him each morning but does that amount to much? Knut adores her. He elevates her to an object of worship and the way he venerates her is unique. *No other woman has a man that takes lingerie or perfumes for her with the intensity and effort I put into treating you. There may be many who get incredible gifts but those gestures are dependent on someone's bank account. What I do with you is completely different.*

Sonia knows it.

She mulls over a tempting idea in her mind for the next few days. See him? Go to Cárdenas and see him? She could take the first flight in the morning and come back on the last one in the evening. That's almost an eight-hour window to spend together. Come in and out of his life, like through a narrow, imperceptible opening. No risks, no commitments. For one day, forget about her mother, her siblings, her grandmother, her husband, her son; forget about her job; forget about the boring men who share music with her she could care less about and ask her out to drinks after work. It's not just the intrigue of seeing Knut that tempts her. More than anything it's the need to pretend, even if it's just for one day, that she can live another life, one in which she plays the role of elegant woman who enjoys being promiscuous and carefree.

Knut doesn't hide his enthusiasm when she proposes it. *I'm moved,* he tells her. *I'll admit that just thinking about it makes me feel a nervousness without precedent . . . But I want to see you, talk to you . . . When you act like this I know anything I can give you is infinitely less than what you deserve.* They set a date. Knut promises he will compensate the travel costs. *They're sufficiently compensated!* she says. *No, really, I mean it. I'll send you something in a few days. I'll see what I can get. I'd love to grab you something you can wear when you come see me.* He doesn't mean lingerie, he rushes to clarify. Some clothes, something refined, sophisticated. He already has a few targets in mind.

A couple of days later he announces the contents of his loot. He can't wait for her to see it all. He needs to tell her all about it. *A black Escada skirt: three almost independent pieces of fabric delicately superimposed, each with a different texture.* He delights in describing it to her. *It's twenty-five and a half inches from the midpoint to the bottom, so it should fit you slightly below the knee. It has some pleats at the top that give it volume but don't take away from the way it hangs. It had been 310 euro but it was on sale for 230.* The process was very easy, he explains, from unsnapping it off the skirt hanger to removing the clip at an empty register, taking advantage of the clerk's distraction. He sends her some pictures, front and back. Sonia examines them closely, but more than the skirt she notices what surrounds it. Knut extended it over a bed—his bed? The comforter has a fading, antiquated floral print with fish that curl around it. In one corner she sees a brown, checkered pillow and a section of a wall painted in pale yellow with remnants of what could've been wallpaper trim. Is that his room? she wonders. She thinks the contrast is strange: an elegant skirt displayed on a cheap comforter. Looking at the picture she realizes that so much conversation about lingerie, restaurants, and literature has obscured his background for her, where he lives. A neighborhood in the outskirts of Cárdenas. She shouldn't forget where he comes from. He and she both come from the same world.

The package will also include a pair of Armani shoes, Knut declares. This time they're a cream color, medium heel, moccasin style, 178 euro. *These you can wear every day*, he says. *I'd love it if you could bring the skirt and these shoes with some thin sheer stockings.* Stockings in the summertime? she says. Of course, why not? He'd like her to always dress like a lady; to go to work with matching skirt and blazer, pearl necklaces, stockings. *And when I say stockings I don't mean pantyhose, like you might think, but authentic stockings, the kind that are held up halfway over your thighs.*

She shouldn't worry if she doesn't have any of those. He's sending a few in different sizes. Since he didn't know which ones would fit her, he took a selection. He almost got caught in one of the stores. When he was about to leave, he saw a camera turning toward him, but he was skillful enough to stay out of its range and leave the merchandise behind before the security guard came over. The guard took him to the back room and searched him thoroughly, but obviously didn't find anything. *I still remember the look of disgust on his face when he took a used napkin out of my jacket pocket.* They let him go and he continued on his hunt in other stores. On the way back home, he saw a young man lying on the ground. He may have slipped on an incline, he'd hit his head on the metal edge of a manhole cover that wasn't properly placed. He was surrounded by people and couldn't move, he looked like an animal that had been run over. He was an ordinary-looking kid, chubby, metal-frame glasses. *I thought God had wanted to punish him while he saved me instants before. He probably approves of me taking those stockings. There's a pair in particular that's quite beautiful, unbeatable; it has a subtle pearl shine. I picture them on your legs . . . I imagine touching the edge, softly posing my hand on it to make sure it stays in place, kissing your knees. It gives me chills.*

Do those kinds of comments bother her? he asks. No, of course not, Sonia replies. On the contrary, actually. She likes them. Then, Knut says, within certain limits, could they plan the fulfillment of a fantasy? How about if she tries on a Tommy Hilfiger shirt he got for her in front of him? Would she do something like that for him? For both of them? She would only have to take off her shirt. He'd like to see one of the La Perla bras on her. *I think my favorite is the black one with the charm hanging between the cups. Could you bring that one, the skirt, the shoes, and the stockings? What do you think? Does it seem like I'm pulling some fantasy business out of the hat as soon as I'm certain that you are coming? Do you find it somewhat perverted or too compromising for you? If you're not clear on how you feel about it, don't worry. I am not asking because I am afraid if you accept we will lose what we have, but to substantiate the fact that I honestly feel as though I already have . . . so much.*

No, that's fine she says. She thinks the shirt plan is almost innocent. Not even her good friend—so reserved and cautious—would label it as problematic.

When she no longer expects it, he sends her a picture. So she can recognize him when they meet, he says. *I find it ridiculous for you to have to guess who I am in the crowd. Let's skip that absurd step.* Sonia inspects the photo, she enlarges it until the pixels stop resembling a human face. She shrinks it back, over and over again. Before her is an average man's face: wide angles and a still overall childish look, darker skin, a good head of hair, a buzz cut. A slight smile, to one side. Thick lips, a small bit of a chipped front tooth visible behind them. Certain pride expressed in the eyes, a bit too close together, and in the slightly raised chin. Thick, black, very dark eyebrows. Sallow skin. Acne? It looks like he has acne or acne scars; the picture isn't sharp enough to tell.

Broad shoulders, somewhat slumped. Height and weight? Not obvious. He's sitting on a cream-colored couch. An old-looking couch. In the background the yellow wall again, textured, not very clean. His house?

The picture doesn't give away much information. There's an enormous distance between that image and the words she reads every day in her inbox. How can she link those incredibly common features with the gifts she's been receiving for years? It's not that she doesn't find the face believable, it's that she couldn't find any face believable.

She goes through the automatic doors, but is so disoriented that she doesn't see him there, standing upright behind the security belt, dressed in a suit despite the warm weather, covered in cologne, with gel on his hair, sweat on his palms, chafing marks on his neck, a small red spot below one of his temples, dead skin peeling off his ears, loaded with shopping bags—two large ones in one hand and a smaller one in the other—looking ahead, palpitating, paralyzed, barely smiling, afraid because she's there and hasn't recognized him. The white lights, the loudspeaker, the crowd of travelers, the images, everything is centrifuged by her bewilderment. She stops briefly, but doesn't manage to make him out in the crowd until he takes a step forward. She blinks surprised, smiles. They say hello with a kiss on each cheek and look down. They walk a few feet and stop. Sonia doesn't know what to say. There's no sign in his face of the expression she saw in the picture—that almost disdainful pride. Instead, she sees shyness, insecurity. He asks her about the flight, his voice is loud and discordant. He shifts his eyes to the sides or slightly down, without looking Sonia in the eye. She's not disappointed because she didn't have any expectations. She has the feeling of being with someone she doesn't know at all. In front of her, a being who breathes, sweats, is agitated, shakes, smiles, looks at her from the corner of his eye. It's true. He exists. He's someone.

Confused, trying to overcome the strange feeling, she returns the smile. He points to her legs.

You brought the skirt.

Sonia straightens it with a downward motion of her hands.

Not the stockings though . . . It's so warm . . .

It looks very good on you. Just like I pictured it. You're very good-looking. Even more so in person. He then looks to the sides, rubs one arm. *Let's get out of here.*

They walk quickly, without speaking. Sonia has a hard time keeping up with his pace. Knut looks straight ahead. She notices the route they're taking isn't improvised. They go up and down ramps, they walk through long halls taking rides on conveyor belts in the direction opposite to the rest of the travelers, dodging carts full of luggage. They finally stop at a corner with two benches that face each other. They sit on the same bench. Sonia stretches her legs and takes a deep breath. Knut shows her the bags.

Go ahead. Look inside. Aren't you curious?

She notices a slight shake in his hands as he opens the bags and takes out the shoes one by one. Each one is carefully wrapped in tissue paper. All are Armani and have high heels and narrow tips, except for a pair of golfing-style flats. The Tommy Hilfiger shirt, made of Lycra with a blue and gray print, is in the smaller bag. Knut watches her, apprehensive. She puts the shirt aside and looks at the shoes. They all still have the price tag, they're all three figures.

I took seven pairs. It was a piece of cake.

There are closed-toe and peep-toe, with strass, with and without ankle straps, studded, and with flashy broguing; formal and cocktail models in black, red, and navy blue; and a pair of brown sandals with yellow straps and silver heels.

I don't know if I can walk in these.

Do you like them? I think they're spectacular.

Sonia spins a pair of sandals in her hands without taking her eye off of them.

Yeah, they're eye-catching.

They're all your size, and the flats you can wear with jeans, to go to the park or grocery shopping with your boy. Those are your style, right?

Sonia lifts her head to confront his face. He's tense, agitated; his eyes are watery, his lips pale and dry. She comes close to his face and kisses him softly on the cheek. She gets a waft of aftershave. *Thank you,* she says in a low voice.

He examines her, perplexed. Swallows saliva.

Don't you want to try them on?

Here?

Sure, no one comes by this spot.

Sonia tries on each pair. She does so quickly and somewhat embarrassed to show her naked feet at the beginning; but she gradually loosens up. Knut asks her to stand up and walk a little. Then to get up on the bench in front of them, so he can get a better perspective. Sonia struggles to keep her balance. She giggles as she wobbles. Knut squints, he contemplates her. He suggests that she wear a pair of the new shoes instead of her sandals.

Any of them would match the skirt. They flatter your legs. Notice your calves. They tense up and harden. It's amazing. You look gorgeous in your outfit, but the heels set you completely apart. Anyone who saw you in those shoes would know you're special. Not just any woman can pull them off.

Sonia hesitates.

But we're going to be walking a lot . . . These could hurt my feet. I think I prefer my sandals if you don't mind.

Knut lowers his head and smiles to himself.

No, I don't mind.

They leave the shoes in a locker and walk around between the airport shops, near the exit. *Do you want to go in somewhere?* he asks. *I can snag you a perfume. Or some lotion. I'd really like for you to see how I do it.*

Sonia smiles. Yes, she'd also love to see. It's more stimulating than trying to force a conversation. She asks him to be careful though. *I wouldn't forgive myself if something happens to you because of me*, she says without too much conviction. Motivated by her comment, Knut raises his voice even more. *If something happens? Nothing will. Really, it's very easy. You'll see for yourself in a minute.*

She watches him from across the entrance of a perfume shop. He has a strong build, his thighs are thick. He's wearing a linen jacket a size or two too small, gray linen pants, a short-sleeved polo shirt, and black dress shoes. She sees him go around the stands a couple of times, try on some cologne here and there, crouch to look at prices in lower shelves. He's back out in five minutes. He signals to her with his head and they walk toward a bench a few hundred feet away. His eyes are shining. His skin looks even more bruised under the direct, artificial airport lighting: peeling, small marks, red spots that spread around his cheeks and forehead. He massages his fingers constantly. Sonia mirrors the motion automatically. She asks him impatiently about what he got. He takes out a gold-colored box from a pocket inside his jacket. He smiles, gives her the box. She tries ripping the plastic wrapper off with her nails, then her teeth. She takes out the perfume bottle nervously.

Incredible, she whispers. *How did you do it? Not even I, who knew, could tell.*

Knut interrupts her. *Wait.* He holds another perfume box in his hands, bigger still: one hundred milliliters. He softly touches the edges of the bottle before extending it to her. The Diors were really easy, he tells her. They didn't even have security stickers.

Sonia takes it, impressed. *Thanks*, she says. She looks to her sides with trepidation.

Can't the cameras see us?

Knut chuckles. No, of course not. Those cameras are hanging there to watch for other things, and many of them don't even work. He's obviously feeling triumphant. Both are delighted; they look directly into each other's eyes, they smile. Sonia puts the perfumes in her purse. They later leave on a bus that takes them to Downtown Cárdenas. They travel standing, holding on to the top handle bar, looking out the window, watching the outskirts of Cárdenas go by: bare fields, an industrial park, the first few urban developments. They turn around and smile at each other every now and then.

Where to now? she asks.

You'll see very soon. I have plans.

Knut had put away the shirt from the smaller bag in his jacket. Neither has commented on it yet.

The entire itinerary has been meticulously scheduled. A tour of malls with more or less quick stops in bookstores and large department stores. She watches him perform with a mix of concern and pride. Knut takes books—two for her son—an Adolfo Domínguez scarf for her, knitted socks imported from Scotland for himself, and juice and cookies for both. All signs of shame in him have disappeared; Sonia notices him relax more each time. He shows her the tags he uses to deactivate the alarms, the way he locates the cameras, and how to recognize incognito security guards. *All you have to do is look. I've never seen worse acting than in their line of work.*

At one of the stores, they visit a La Perla section. It's so crowded that Knut acknowledges, displeased, how difficult it will be to grab anything. Sonia is surprised so many people can afford to spend that much money on lingerie. She overhears a salesclerk bending over backward to help a couple picking clothing for their honeymoon. Both are tanned and look like they're in their mid-forties, they speak in a loud voice, attracting attention. The clerk shows them specific pieces and they giggle pointing at the revealing parts in each piece, feeling the fabrics, holding them up against the light. Sonia thinks the scene is ridiculous and obscene. Two other couples, one of them quite young, look at nightgowns casually, without checking the prices. Knut gestures for them to walk out to a different store where, in two minutes, he seizes a satin Lise Charmel robe. He later points at a woman of about fifty who's there with her daughter—the girl's face has hints of the mother's features, yet to be expressed. Knut focuses on the mother, not the daughter. Her volumized hair is dyed light blonde, she's wearing a tight dress, and black shoes with very high heels. Her cold attitude reminds Sonia a little of Tippi Hedren.

Notice the difference from the others.

Sonia looks straight at her.

I'm not sure what you mean. You do realize she's had plastic surgery, right? Look at her lips, they're completely swollen . . . And her expression . . . It's like it's frozen.

Knut keeps looking at her, dazzled.

I think plastic surgery is great.

Sonia becomes impatient, crosses her arms in front of her, looks around, shows contempt.

Whatever you say. I need to use the restroom.

They wander around the cosmetics section next. Sonia signals to show Knut what she wants and he puts it in his pockets: two small bottles of nail polish, a moisturizer, lipstick, a face mask. This Corte Inglés has many more cosmetics stands than the one in her city, she thinks. All sorts of products suddenly become irresistible. She starts picking them with childlike enthusiasm, the same enthusiasm Knut shows in pleasing her.

If you lived here, we could do this more often, he says.

I don't think we could stop ourselves.

The Sephora clerk comes by to offer Sonia a free makeup session. While she explains how Sonia's supposed to apply the products, Knut browses around the displays. Sitting on a high chair, as the young woman in front of her brushes powders on her face, Sonia sees how he snags a StriVectin cream. The large, fluorescent-color sign reads, *"Better than Botox?"* He takes the jar, pastes a sticker on it and puts in in his jacket pocket. Anyone looking could've seen him do it.

But no one was looking, he tells her once she's finished. *I made sure beforehand. I never improvise.*

We have enough, anyway. We've been walking around for a good while.

Knut chuckles, he squints slightly.

Are you worried? he says, endeared by her.

Yeah, a little. Let's go. I've got all sorts of things. Really.

They start walking toward the exit and Sonia sees him look up very subtly. The muscles in his face contract; he flushes immediately.

What is it?

He doesn't answer. She follows him, docile, without asking again. A man in uniform with a walkie-talkie speaks with his mouth against the device. Sonia sees him from the corner of her eye and immediately looks down. She starts feeling dizzy. Her legs become loose, she's nauseous. She slows down. Knut's voice rescues her from the trance.

Don't stop.

The sound of the walkie-talkie vibrates behind them, then a beep, and a dry *copy.* Yet no one stops them. The automatic doors open smoothly. They walk through. They're hit by the hot, still noon air. The sidewalk shines under the sun. A huge parking lot extends in front of them. An elderly man in the distance moves with effort using a walker. A slow pace replaces the earlier agitation. They walk a few feet; then Knut stops and faces her.

Can I hug you?

Sonia nods. They hug. She finds his body oddly relaxed. He holds her but he's looking to the side, in the direction of one of the eaves of the building they just left. He puts his hands on her shoulders, looks her in the eye, comes close again, and kisses her mouth. Sonia kisses him back. They hug again. They kiss like that for some time. Knut keeps looking toward the building now and then. Sonia's also thinking of something else.

Later, in the restaurant where he'd made a reservation, Knut explains what was happening.

There was a camera on us. But they must've not been sure. That's why they didn't even stop us to ask.

Yes, they also put cameras on the outside. One was focusing on them while they were kissing in the parking lot. He liked doing it there, precisely for that reason. *They were probably so confused.*

He scoops all the ice cream out of the second cup he's ordered and leans back against the chair. Before, after a thorough inspection of the silverware, he'd eaten a brownie, crème brûlée, and three glasses of water he had to order one by one.

If they'd bring a pitcher like I always ask them . . .

Sonia takes another sip of her beer. Next to it is the plate she's barely touched. She casually checks the time. The restaurant is teeming with customers; the waitress gets to the tables as she can. The service is slow and the atmosphere overwhelming. Sonia observes the other tables. A woman about her age converses enthusiastically with a man in his fifties. A serious, elegant-looking couple eats with extreme focus, barely speaking. Four men laugh loudly and interrupt each other in the smoking section. Knut calls the waitress, who rushes her way across the room and mumbles an excuse. He asks her for a moist towel to wash his hands again. Sonia watches him closely as he rubs them, she sees his furrowed eyebrows, the pointed tip of his lips—perhaps the only feature that gives his face some uniqueness. He leans forward again and moves the plate away to extend his arm across the table. They take each other's hand. They look at their hands for a minute or two as they interlace their fingers. Knut's hands are only slightly bigger than hers. His fingernails are neatly cut, very clean. She, however, has bitten fingernails and her cuticles aren't manicured, she has hangnails, bits of peeling, and cuts.

That's a symptom of an unstable nature, he says.

Sonia takes back her hand.

Don't get mad. My skin is also wrecked. As you can obviously tell, it peels and gets red constantly. I get pimples and eczema; and I have a cold sore on my lip that flares up every winter. But for you it would be easy to avoid your hands looking like that. I'd like to help you be well.

She shrugs.

What's the plan now? It's getting late.

Knut seems to consider the question for a moment. He tilts his head slightly, brushes the tips of his fingers on his lips.

We'll go somewhere so you can try on the shirt. Like we talked about.

A dressing room?

No. There's an office building nearby that I'm familiar with. A guy who buys videogames from me works there. No one goes to the top.

What do you mean by the top?

I mean the stairs, the hallway. The very last room on the top floor, the one that leads to the roof. No one goes up there, not even the guard.

Alright, she says. They look at each other in silence.

Not until after they pay the check, he leans toward her ear and asks: *Are you wearing any of the La Perla bras?*

The departure screen announces the gate is now open for pre-boarding. They get up and stand next to each other without saying anything.

I have to get going.

Knut grazes her arm. He looks inconsolably defeated, like

the weight of the world just fell on him. His touch is almost unbearable; she doesn't move away, but she looks straight at the floor. She can hear his breath become agitated next to her. He softly removes a hair on her shirt. *Can I keep it?* he asks her. *Sure,* she says. She comes close, hugs him. She notices the stiffness in his tense body. Knut lets out a slight, almost inaudible, pant. They kiss one last time. She steps back, takes all the bags, and walks away without looking back.

She leaves the bags with the shoes and the new loot in her trunk. The airport parking lot is almost empty, as is the highway. Sonia drives distractedly. Another car's emergency lights on the shoulder of the road shake up her lethargy. What an ordeal to go through in the middle of the night, she thinks. The driver is standing next to the open hood of her car, wearing a reflective jacket, immobilized. Their eyes cross when Sonia's car passes her. Sonia sees her afflicted, expectant expression. She tries not to think about it.

She parks and opens the trunk again. She takes out the books for her son, rearranges the bags, and puts a mat over them.

Verdú welcomes her sleepily. The only light in the room is coming from the TV screen. A green tone from a sequence occurring in a forest is reflected on the wall. Sonia's eyes itch. She drops down on the couch and leans her head on Verdú's shoulder. He puts his arm around her, kisses her temple.

Tired?

Dead.

Do you want dinner?

She shakes her head no.

I'd have a drink.

Verdú holds her chin in his two fingers and turns her head so their eyes meet.

Sonia, we said no more drinks during the week. At least during the week. That's what we said.

She sighs and scratches her eyes.

I need to unwind. You have no idea what today was like. They took us everywhere. It was nonstop, meeting after meeting.

And you didn't drink there?

Of course not. I never drink at work functions. It's not that hard to understand, is it? That after being out for fifteen hours a person comes home and wants to have a quiet drink. A fucking drink. I'm not asking for more.

Verdú gets up, he examines her.

OK, I'll make you a gin and tonic. But it'll be a light one. And you're only having one.

She nods and collapses on the couch. She closes her eyes, unbuttons her skirt, throws it on the floor.

Well, well, says Verdú when he comes back.

Don't get the wrong idea. I couldn't wait to take it off. It's too tight on my waist. It's so uncomfortable.

Well it'll get dirty there. I'm afraid the floor isn't very clean.

I don't care. I don't think I'll ever wear it again.

When the years go by and I have to remember what happiness was for me, I'll surely think of the moments from the time the plane landed until I suddenly saw you come out in the crowd. At first he thought she didn't recognize him. He even feared for a moment that she had regretted the whole idea and was going to keep walking to avoid him. *My heart was beating so fast!* But then she looked at him and smiled. *Now, I try to relive those instants every night.*

Sonia closes the email. What can she reply? She already answered all his questions. Now they have to analyze every detail of the encounter, point by point. *Did you like kissing me?* Yes, he's a very good kisser. *Did you feel uncomfortable when you tried on the shirt?* No, not at all. It was a nice moment. Intense. Special. *Was it fun to keep me company in my expeditions?* Of course, it was fun in addition to unique . . . it's not an everyday thing to do; she can appreciate that. *What did her son say about the books?* He liked them. *Has Verdú seen any of the shoes?* No, not yet. She'll have to find a way of taking them out without him suspecting anything. *And the robe? Does it fit you well?* Yes, perfectly. *Will there ever be a day, even if it's a long time from now, when we can repeat what we lived together?* Sure there will be. *Would you want to repeat it?* Absolutely.

After a short time she receives another package. *It's simply fair that I compensate you for the wonderful day you gave me. And this doesn't even start to cover it,* he says. A white Armani jacket. Sonia checks the price tag and is almost not impressed anymore: 499 euro. How did he manage to get such an expensive piece of clothing? she asks him. She realizes there's been a progression to the gifts, the increasing level of surprise has kept her hooked and expectant until now. First it was the books, to which the records were added. Then the perfumes started coming. When there were too many he sent a bra, which has been followed with all kinds of lingerie; then shoes, lotion, designer clothes . . . When the excitement starts to wear off by force of habit, something novel arrives. Where does it end?

She shouldn't worry, he insists. The jacket's an exceptional piece: it *had* to be for her. He'd like it if she wore it buttoned up with nothing underneath, no bra, like the model in the catalog picture he sends her. Since the top button is quite low, a good portion of the girl's breasts is visible. *The insinuation of an offer that isn't anything yet,* Knut says. *But I don't have that model's body,* says Sonia. *It doesn't matter,* he insists. *I'm convinced it will look splendid on you.*

Sonia doesn't know what to do with the jacket now. She tries it on like he suggested, but the effect is completely different than the catalog picture: she just looks partially undressed, like if she threw the jacket on for a minute to get up and open the door. She tries it on with a black blouse underneath and a skirt. She looks in the mirror, furrows her brow. No. She just put on ten years. She tries again with a colorful shirt, jeans, and flats. She turns around. She buttons it. It bulges up on the sides. It's too tight on her chest. And that color, she thinks. A white jacket. Is she supposed to like it just because it's 500 euro? Because of the brand? No. She's supposed to like it because Knut took it for her. Because he put himself at risk for her. Because he's fantasized about her, and now he expects her to confirm his expectations.

Sonia gives up on trying to convince him. Yes, she tells him. She loves it. It's very flattering. She tries to keep it in a bag, it gets too wrinkled when she folds it. She can't hang it in her closet, she can't wear it, she can't even give it as a gift—to whom? What would they think? She still has the seven pairs of shoes in the trunk of her car, plus the ones she's hiding in the back of the closet. She's keeping all the lingerie in a box, she has the perfumes from long ago that she hasn't worn, the creams, the stockings . . . It's too much, she tells herself, it's too much.

She sits on the edge of the bed, pensive. She then gets up abruptly, takes the jacket and throws it in a trash bag.

She stops three feet away from the garbage bin outside and turns around.

She just had a better idea.

The listing price is 299 euro. *Armani jacket, current season, size 38, deeply discounted. Take advantage of this chance to own a couture-like piece for a lot less.* She attaches the picture with the model that Knut sent, and lists the details of all the measurements. At first, she logs in to her account every half hour to follow the progress, she opened it under a pseudonym. She soon finds out it won't be as easy as she expected. Days go by and no one bids. When the ad is almost expired, she lowers the price even more. *199 euro. Amazing chance. Don't miss out!* She doesn't get bids this time either. She lowers it again, to 120 euro, and this time she gets the first inquiry. Is the product authentic?

a woman asks. Can she send a real picture? Yes, of course it's authentic. She may return it if she's not satisfied when she sees it. The jacket is a beauty, it's an investment she'll have in her closet the rest of her life. She secretly borrows Verdú's camera and photographs the garment she's worked hard to extend over the table. She also takes a picture of the tag and uploads it to the ad. The woman doesn't make up her mind after all that. On eBay, where falsifications abound, comments and ratings from previous customers are very important. Sonia doesn't have any.

A month later, after successive reductions in price, she's able to sell it for 49 euro, including shipping costs. The jacket makes its way to its new destination in a small package that Sonia, relieved, finally mails. Days later the first comment shows up on her account. The customer highlights eagerly the legitimacy of the transaction and speed of the shipment. Sonia feels glad. She thinks this may make future sales easier.

Meanwhile Knut has been sending her more gifts: another stack of books—*when will you write more stories again?* he insists—a new perfume—*it was terribly easy, I know you have a lot, but keep it for later*—a La Perla lace bralette—*very Dita Von Teese*—fishnet stockings—*idem*—a Tous handkerchief— *wild silk, just the name sounds promising*—a collapsible Burberry umbrella—*so you can always have it in your purse*. Sonia gives the perfume bottle to her mom and sells the rest in batches. Many people still don't trust the authenticity of the items and don't take a chance on bidding unless she lowers the price significantly, which in turn makes them distrust even more. Still, she's able to market quite a few perfumes, four pairs of shoes, and some stockings, for less than a sixth of their original price. The lingerie is impossible to sell though, even if she practically gives it away. She spends much time answering emails, preparing shipments, and staying on top of the expiration dates of the ads. She periodically receives small deposits in her checking account, nothing that substantially changes her life.

One day she suggests to Verdú that they go out of town for the weekend. They could rent a place near the beach, she says. Their son would love a change of pace. It's been too long since they broke the monotony.

It'll be my treat, she says smiling. *I've been saving a little.*

Verdú looks up from the newspaper, purses his lips, wrinkles his chin.

In just one second she can tell how much disdain the gesture expresses. A window swings pushed by the wind, rhythmically hitting the frame—it's a gray, intemperate day. This is the sound she'll remember when she tries to make sense of the entire scene later on.

What's wrong? she asks.

This is when Verdú brings up divorce.

Knut notices she's been distant. She doesn't explain why. *Your attitude has been evasive, withdrawn lately*, he tells her. I go through phases, she says, just moments that eventually pass. She admits her mood is low, but it has nothing to do with him. It's the inertia of repetition, she says, all the days are the same, it weighs her down, immobilizes her. *You should quit your job*, he suggests. *I know I can be insistent but you're not meant to be stuck in an office. You should be devoted to writing, nothing else. Maybe I can help you achieve it.*

Again with that? she thinks. It isn't amusing for her to entertain the idea right now. It doesn't even upset her. All she feels is a slight irritation that doesn't quite become a nuisance. She simply doesn't argue with him. She tells him yes, she wishes she could leave it all behind—and for her, *all* means something completely different than what Knut has in mind—but she never actually contemplates real possibilities. Knut proposes that she make a list of the items she needs in her everyday life. He can steal them and ship them to her, it would save Sonia some costs. *I realize this wouldn't take care of all of your needs but it would cover some. Maybe with my contribution you can at least ask to be scheduled fewer hours per week at work. Why don't we at least test it? Let me try.*

A list? Is he going to go from store to store crossing off the products as he's able to get them? That must be very tiring, Sonia says. She doesn't think it's worth it. Plus, what she needs is too mundane: toilet paper, detergent, legumes, light bulbs, notebooks, things like that. He must have better things to do than waste his time with her grocery shopping. Knut reiterates it isn't a problem. *We'll obviously include articles in the list that are easy to ship, so the shipping cost doesn't cut into the amount you'd be saving. The light bulbs and notebooks, for example, I would definitely be able to send you. Think about expensive items that don't weigh too much. Anything can be obtained. It wouldn't take me that long and, besides that, I have all the time in the world; time is precisely what I have in my life.*

8. THE LIST

COLORED PENCILS, THE notebooks her son was asked to bring on his first day in grade school, watercolors, notepads, seventeen books for Italian class (from manuals to dictionaries to collected readings) a computer mouse, a DVD tower, tampons, kitchen scissors, two colanders (six and eight inches), hair mask, insect killer, replacement bulbs for insect killer, hand cream, acetone nail-polish remover, sunblock (for children and adults), floss, lip balm, brewer's yeast pills, valerian pills, vacuum-sealed ham, pine nuts, Playmobil toy figures, Bratz dolls for Elena, silver cleaner, videogames for Lucas, socks, sole inserts, spools of thread in several colors, makeup brushes.

In addition, everything that Knut includes of his own accord, which Sonia accepts without too much resistance. Two pairs of Tous gloves: leather and wool, a Donna Karan scarf. Armani ballerinas. A complete facial treatment by RoC. Bronzing spray for her legs. A La Perla bathing suit. More stockings. Calvin Klein satin-silk pajamas with shorts and a lace top. A Purificación García handbag. A small Hugo Boss neck handkerchief. Books (short stories by Nabokov, Juan José Saer, Javier Tomeo, Benet). Music (he's into Jordi Savall lately). Also an MP3 player and a new cell phone.

Sonia sells the Tous gloves (just the leather ones), the scarf (she hates that the letters DKNY are printed on it), the Armani ballerinas (she wouldn't have worn them under any circumstance), and the handbag on eBay (she finds the strass completely opposite to her style).

9. AROUND THE SAME TIME

Which role do you think
each of us plays in this relationship?
Sometimes I feel like we play mother and son;
sometimes father and daughter. Being
siblings would be alright too, if we didn't have to
worry about incest restrictions.
What's clear to me is that our relationship,
for better or for worse, can never be "normal."

VERDÚ IS NOW a fabrication. Sonia uses his fictitious presence as a boundary, as protection against the overflowing fantasy—which overflows for Knut too. Her mood swings and sadness persist. Loneliness, at times, bites insistently. Sonia has turned thirty: she can look back and trace the circuitous path she's left behind, but she can't perceive an exit. The emptiness her grandmother left after dying is larger than she could've imagined. Her family has always claimed—and it was repeated during the funeral—that she's an exact copy of her. Their physical appearance is nearly identical, but also their personality, they say. Sonia still keeps the picture of her sitting on a blanket; it's old and burnt on the edges. She looks at the young woman in the photo—younger than she is now. *I hope so*, she says. Her grandmother's intense gaze in the picture has a staggering purity. She's gleaming with a wonder that Sonia thinks she's lost a long time ago. When did everything start to get tangled? she asks herself.

The fantasy expands to fill the holes. Knut and her each have their own, Sonia reflects. She believes these empty spaces that they have in common bring them closer. She doesn't always think this, of course; but when she does, it's from the illogical point of view of desperation.

Fantasy grows and eats away at them. It gains density and weight.

Fantasizing becomes a necessity for both. They do it daily. The difference is Sonia is able to forget the next day. Knut isn't. Knut doesn't forget anything. For him, everything accumulates.

She photographs herself again wearing a couple of lingerie sets in front of the mirror. Low-quality images of an attractive dimness that she does send him this time, after editing them to pixelate her face. He reacts with enthusiasm. He tells her she's stunning. Yet it isn't the pictures themselves he finds erotic. His fascination is born from the indirect. More than the pictures, he's aroused by the memory of the bus ride they took from the airport to Downtown Cárdenas. Sonia had grabbed on to the handlebar to move along the aisle and he saw a hint of sweat on her armpit. *A simple detail, sure, but how does that almost biblical quote from Hamlet go? The one that says providence can be found even in the fall of a sparrow? We got on the bus just so I could realize how much I wanted you. Particularly, how much I wanted to kiss your arms, sweat included.*

He's aroused by the hair that she shed and that he keeps in his wallet. The shirt she tried on in front of him. How the newly seized clothes feel to the touch. The careful packing of the boxes. Insinuations and fragments of insinuations.

What do you imagine with me?

They both take refuge in each other, they console each other.

They fantasize about the possibility of seeing each other again. Would it be possible to spend the night together sometime? Knut asks. Does she think it's foreseeable? *Speaking modestly, I think I deserve to see you with the white stockings, the brown shoes . . . and nothing else. The black bralette with the fishnet stock-ings, the first pair of red shoes . . . and nothing else. The tunic and those same red shoes. The white garter with the white stockings and one of the white bras. The flower-pattern set you say fits you so well and the dotted stockings.* When he says he wants to see her, he insists, he means strictly to see. The spell would break perma-nently if it were more than that. *We should never give in to the primary impulse. That's how I prefer it.*

It's Sonia who proposes that they set a date. How about a year from now? she suggests. *That way we could prove to ourselves that it's still something we want, that it isn't just a spur-of-the-moment idea.* Knut replies that he has nothing to prove to himself. *You're afraid of the consequences of your fickleness and you're right to be prudent, but as far as my position goes, I have no doubts whatsoever.* The one-year proposal seems fine to him though. He actually prefers to have all that time to fantasize. It's always the proposition itself that arouses him.

What could we do? they ask each other often. *I'd like both of us to decide what pieces and shoes you'd bring with you.* What does she think fits her the best? She could bring the most comfortable ones to wear in the hotel. He mentions past gifts that she sold months ago—a skirt, several pairs of shoes, a blouse. Sonia trusts he'll forget. There are so many clothes to choose from, so many she hasn't worn yet. It's absurd to worry about that now, the meeting day is far ahead, she tells him. If it even happens at all, she tells herself. She doesn't really ever believe any of it.

What else could we do? Kiss, yes, they did that before and liked it, right? They'll kiss again then: on the cheek, on the lips, kiss each other's hair. She should let him slowly kiss her legs with the stockings on, from her ankles to her hips . . . *pose my lips on your hair, feel your pelvis protruding under one of the garters, slide my fingers between the straps, the buckles . . .* He'd also like to give soft, very slow kisses to the shoes while she wears them. *I could spend the entire night doing that.* This isn't a break from their initial boundaries, he clarifies. He won't touch her directly. He wouldn't dare. He assures her he'll show her reverential respect. He uses the word *extreme*. He does, however, want to see her half-naked, wild, elegant. *Lioness.*

Sonia finds the catalog of fantasies he presents both attractive and perturbing. Knut makes sure to clarify the details, to express the subtlety in the ambiguity. He likes to imagine the moment in the airport when he'll come pick her up. *You walk toward me wearing the white Armani jacket buttoned up with nothing underneath, no bra. Your breasts move slightly as you take each step, your nipples protrude. You're wearing the same black skirt you had on last time, without any underwear. Just a garter with stockings and a splendid-looking pair of high heels. The skirt's silk sticks delicately to the contours of your pubic mound. The triangle outline it forms is wildly arousing. Nothing is visible, but anyone can tell you're nearly naked under the skirt and jacket.* If she allows it, they could find a nook to hide in and be alone for a few minutes. Sonia could lift her skirt a little, spread the fabric apart, maybe caress herself while he contemplates her.

Knut constructs the scenes with endless insinuations. He can write an entire paragraph describing his thigh muscles tensing, but he employs omission to express the rest. Everything is delicate, suggestive, and profoundly deviant at the same time.

They plan the meeting with convincing concreteness. They compare specific hotels, for example. They discuss prices, locations, and are confronted with each other's tastes. All the hotels he suggests are expensive and sophisticated, but also cold and anonymous—most are on the outskirts of the city or in the business district. *I admit it would turn me on very much to stay in a hotel that's hosting a convention for business executives and to run into some of them during breakfast; to watch them look at you full of desire and watch you glance back arrogantly; to witness that entire courtship.* She should bring a suitcase full of the most enticing lingerie gifts, even if it's only a day trip. *Or rather, all of the ones that fit you well. It doesn't matter that there won't be enough time for you to wear them all.* It's not about wearing them all in front of him, but about Sonia and him picking out outfits together and her changing in the bathroom while he waits, looking at the rest of the lingerie spread out on the bed. *I'd actually like you to take a long time changing; the wait would build the anticipation.*

He describes the possible variants, from the outfits she'd wear—the fuchsia corset and black stockings . . . or the beige lace one-piece with the blue shoes . . . or the corset with the red garters, and the ribbon stockings—to the setting of the scene—her lying on a couch . . . her in front of a mirror . . . him standing while she sits . . . him lying down while she stands—and what they would do next—only look . . . or touch themselves separately looking each other in the eye . . . or whisper obscenities in each other's ear without performing them.

Although the erotic tone of his fantasies increases, Knut continues to use euphemisms. He tells her, for example, that one possible form of consummation would be for him to *finish* on her body, without ever touching her. He could take a picture of *the result* without capturing their faces. Given his evident inability to *do it* directly with her, another possibility is to watch her *doing it* with someone else, preferably a younger man, almost a boy, like if she were teaching him. Knut would limit himself to looking; and she, well, she could look back at him tenderly.

When he sends those kinds of propositions to her and doesn't get an answer, he's caught in a state of anguish and remorse. He immediately thinks he's gone too far and Sonia's gotten upset, although she rushes to say no. Why doesn't she tell him what she'd like to do then? It's not enough to listen or agree and then not contribute anything. *If you don't reciprocate my disclosures I feel unsafe, not only in relation to you, but to the entirety of the world.* He's never revealed any single portion of these fantasies, however small, to anyone before—not even to himself: isn't that proof of how pure his feelings are?, of everything he's willing to do for her?, of how much he really loves her? He's always been uncomfortable talking about sex. Even reading about it. *I felt attracted to Joyce's and Nora's work but rejected it,* he says. Not to mention certain Beckett fragments. And Faulkner? Doesn't his work too depict lasciviousness, brutality, and incest? Does she recall Agota Kristof's books? Jerzy Kosinski's? How about Elfriede Jelinek's? They're, of course, scandalous to the societies they're exposing. What is sex if not an accusation? She, who likes film so much, what does she have to say about the significance of Bergman and Buñuel? What about Pasolini? She shouldn't be scared to share her fantasies. Every word he writes has a back side. *Look behind them,* he tells her, *you'll find me there waiting for you, trembling, insecure.*

Does he really want to know what she wants? In one of her days of rage and loneliness, Sonia writes a cruel response not knowing whether she wants to stimulate him or push him away. She'd like him to treat her with detachment, she says, roughly, even. To use her to satisfy himself without so much paraphernalia and sophistication. That's what he does with the others, isn't it? Why can't he do it with her too? He replies: precisely because he does it with the others. He tells her that this desire of hers to be used, her profound rejection of *something* he'll dare call *respect*—if the word *love* seems excessive—must be rooted in her childhood where, as she knows, everything originates. *You want to be used like Deneuve in* Belle de Jour *because that would allow you to be cold when you need to be. Others' cruelty will justify yours in the future. It's a way for you to protect yourself from the fear you feel when I give myself to you. That's why you responded like that. I simply don't buy it.*

Right around that time, Knut meets another woman of about forty-something. He starts going out with her often. Sonia asks for more details. What's she like? What about her does he find attractive? He tells her she lives in a different city but doesn't say which one. It's not far, an hour away by train, but she's the one who goes to Cárdenas to see him. *I'm very immobile as you know.* He met her online. At first they'd chat all day, although their conversations were intermittent and superficial, probably because she was chatting with other men at the same time. Knut once accused her of having an Internet addiction, which she angrily denied until she had no choice but to admit it. Six hours a day online are too many, she said, she spends four or five at most. When Knut proved to her with a detailed record of chat logs that it was indeed six hours, and sometimes more, she asked him who he thought he was to monitor her, and said that he, more than anyone, should shut up because that meant he also spent the day online. *Aside from the fact that comforting ourselves by comparing our actions to those of others is rather weak and never excuses our behavior, my situation isn't like hers. The only person I spend the day online with is you, but our relationship transcended the Internet realm long ago.*

M., how he refers to her, contradicts herself continuously, she doesn't use logic, she's lazy, fickle, chaotic. *Those are the same faults you see in me!* Sonia points out. No, he answers: those are feminine traits that manifest in different ways in each woman. That's why, as opposed to Sonia, who inspires veneration in him, M. brings out a decidedly sadistic instinct. He didn't want to go out with her because he was attracted to her at all, but for exactly the opposite reason: because he felt repulsion. Scientific interest, he adds. He admits he likes to censure her because it's a way to censure himself.

She isn't physically appealing either. *She claims to be either the rebel, or the hippie, or the black sheep of a well-to-do family, which is supposed to justify that shabby look of hers . . .* Unkempt hair, cheap clothes . . . Her eyes are always watery, like she's just sneezed. She chain-smokes, which has taken a toll on her skin—it's yellow—and her teeth— they're stained. *The first time*

I saw her, her hair looked like she hadn't washed it in weeks. This isn't a personal criticism. If you, me, Greta Garbo, Paul Auster, or whoever, don't wash our hair in a month, it would also be disgusting. To help her become aware of this, he mentioned to her that it was starting to fall out, mostly in the middle, from lack of hygiene. She said he was wrong, it actually grew nonstop. *"Look, look. Touch right here. I had to cut it myself the other day cause it's been growing so much,"* she insisted, taking his arm. *The day she goes bald she'll be convinced she has a lion's mane. Is it better not to say anything? Is it preferable to settle into a false compassion than to point these things out, however inconvenient? If my perception isn't correct then there isn't any risk of hurting her and, if I'm right, she should take my observations as opportunities to improve, since it doesn't harm her in any way for someone to call attention to the things she can't see.*

He's also noticed something odd about the way she walks. *Like she's hanging from her shoulders; with an odd rhythm that isn't appealing from afar—at all.* Her movements are like an infant's wobbles when it's learning to walk, with the difference that in a woman her age it looks strange. He suggested she use arch support but he's afraid her walk has more to do with all those anti-anxiety pills she takes. *I'm not a shining example of graceful walking either, but in men a strange walk is associated with having a strong personality. So much so, that it used to be considered a mark of the devil and sometimes it was attributed a demonic uniqueness, like in Stalin's case.* She always seems to be thinking of something very important, something that won't let her live. *So, as you walk with her it looks like you're dragging her someplace she doesn't want to go. You say something to her, and she keeps smoking, looks down at the ground with an expression of disgust on her face, and after about half a minute, when she feels like it, she answers.*

The day they met for the first time, M. told him she had a lover—first she said *boyfriend*, then *lover* because at her age, she clarified, one doesn't have *boyfriends* anymore. She also said they had chosen to be free. Knut asked if that meant they were able to have other relationships simultaneously. Yes, yes, exactly. She bowed her head to say yes as if it were too heavy. *Her cervical vertebrae must be mush with all that wobbling.*

They had lunch in a fairly expensive restaurant. *She paid. Not very happily, although I promised to compensate her immediately.* When she took out her ID to put it next to her credit card, Knut confirmed his suspicion: she was a couple of years older than she had told him. He pointed it out, and her reaction was limited to a sad smile.

They went to several malls where he grabbed a perfume, a shirt, two lotions, and four movies. *All together it amounted to much more than the price of the meal, but she still didn't seem satisfied.* They spent the entire afternoon at the malls and then had dinner late in the evening at a leisurely pace, even though the last train to her city left before eleven. As the time drew closer, Knut would remind her they'd better get going. She wouldn't get ready. She wanted to have the last smoke, and the last one, and the last one. Knut insisted after a few minutes. M. signaled to the waiter to get the check but he walked right by and she just sat there, pensive. They finally left the restaurant with just enough time. He told her if she took a cab to the train station she could still make it. She didn't seem to care about missing the train. She gave him an indecisive look, and suggested they go to an inn. *The average person might hear the story and think I prolonged the meal on purpose and pressured her to drink, like in a classic villain vs. victim tale.* But Knut told M. he wouldn't set foot in an inn, not even with Ava Gardner herself. Inns in that area of town were about forty or fifty a night. For eighty-five they could stay in an acceptable four-star hotel. M. thought it was a good plan. As they began to walk, he asked her, not without blushing, if she had any condoms. No, she answered. Knut didn't have any either. *Like I said, I hadn't planned it.* M.

went into a drugstore to buy them while he waited outside. It took her at least twenty minutes. He passed the time watching the parade of women who are out of his reach: *incredible-looking Americans, exquisitely attractive partygoers walking in groups, women walking alone, girls with several young men, couples . . .*

The hotel was full. The young woman at the front desk mentioned that on a Friday night without a reservation it would be difficult to find a vacancy. M. babbled about the possibility of going to an inn again. It didn't make a difference, inns would probably be full as well, said the front desk agent. Once they were out the door, shivering from the cold, Knut mentioned a 170-euro, five-star hotel to M., thinking this would make her give up. He even told her that for less than that she could take a cab to her city. *I felt sorry about rejecting her, but I still wasn't feeling like doing it.* Several taxis drove by and still she hadn't made up her mind. They walked in silence and sat on a bench. M. continued to chain-smoke. She turned to face him and confessed she was feeling guilty about her boyfriend. But hadn't she said they had agreed to give each other freedom for this kind of thing? he asked. Still, she insisted, she felt guilty. She just felt guilty, she just felt guilty, she kept repeating. Okay, Knut said, they wouldn't do anything then. He got up ready to leave and she took his hand. She begged him to stay. She wasn't going to feel guilty then? Knut asked. No, no. She just had a moment of doubt, she's clear now. Knut asked her to think it through, because he was a man after all, and if she changed her mind later, he wouldn't be able to. He explained to her that people who change their mind often, do so in both directions, so she could regret it the next day. She wouldn't respond. She would just stare at him.

At four in the morning they were finally in the five-star hotel room. It took them a while to get started. He liked her breasts, which were larger and better than he had expected, but he was bothered by three particular things: she wouldn't stop

smoking—the air in the room soon became unbreathable—
she was wearing a pad—*looking at that manifestation of your
aberrant physiology should be included in Buddhist exercises to
ward off desire*—and her armpits weren't shaved. In different
circumstances, this last detail may have even aroused him. He
pictures Sonia, for example, and realizes how much he'd love to
see her with hair, but in M. it was proof of unpreparedness and
lack of hygiene.

They were only able to *do it* after a long while. Before going
to sleep, Knut mentioned the torture of Savonarola, a sudden
thought he had about repentance due to desperation. Since she
wasn't responding, he turned on the night lamp next to the
bed, looked her in the eye, and asked her to honestly tell him if
she knew who he was talking about. M. let out a tired *"Yeah."*
Knut begged her to prove it by telling him everything she knew
about Savonarola. She giggled and said that she gets the facts
mixed up, that she was tired, and that it was time to go to sleep.
They slept for two or three hours. In the morning, Knut stuffed
himself with sweet pastries and juice from the breakfast buffet
while he read the newspaper. He suggested to her that if they
charged her for breakfast, she say that the front desk agent from
the previous night had said it was included in the room price.
The lie worked. *That receptionist must have gotten an earful.
Nothing that wasn't planned in the universal order. He was quite
the unpleasant man, by the way.*

M., whom he now speaks about every day, becomes Knut's new
obsession. In his emails he alternates between compliments for
Sonia and contempt for her, as if he were comparing them. He
describes, for example, how awful the lingerie looks on her.
*When she wears them, the sets go from looking suggestive to . . . com-
pletely ridiculous.* Maybe that's just what happens when fantasy
meets reality, Sonia suggests. *Don't think it'll be very different
with me.* Knut's expectations of her are too high, she tells him.

So high, they make her feel insecure. He describes his vision of the lingerie and her body with such precision that she's afraid to disappoint him. The lingerie on her looks like it would on the average person, and of course, not nearly as good as it does on the models on the tags. The pictures she sent him were deceiving, in the sense that they flattered her; she picked them to be flirtatious. Nothing will be as perfect as he thinks, and she'll end up turning into another M. for him.

Knut tries to reassure her. He promises her that no man will ever want her like he wants her. He's not referring to the intensity, but to the way. What he's been attracted to ever since he sent her the first bra is her behavior toward the lingerie—it's spontaneous. If her behavior had been different, he wouldn't have sent another piece; but she did exactly what she was supposed to do: receive it with enthusiasm, tell him how it looked on her, understand his impulse, and not only not censor it, but encourage it. *Just like I told you that I don't mind if the stories you write are imperfect, because I know that with your talent they will be one day, I can tell you that you seduce me with your attitude toward the lingerie, the same attitude that motivated me to send you many more sets, and the same attitude that eventually prompted you to choose the best ones to wear and take a picture—something that M. would never do, for example. Remember when you changed shirts and I mentioned your scar? Do you think I mind? Quite the opposite: you don't know what I would give to have the courage to kiss it. Your flirtatiousness isn't causing any disappointment in me, in fact I consider it an accomplishment. You instinctively act exactly in the way that arouses me the most.*

To show her what he means, he forwards her a picture M. had sent to him. It's an out-of-focus self-portrait in which she's wearing excessive makeup and looks old, ugly, tired. Her murky eyes are looking directly at the camera but she seems to be thinking about something else. A mess is visible behind her: cardboard file boxes thrown on a shelf, an unmade bed, dirty dishes every-where on the floor. *See? I wasn't exaggerating.* It isn't the image itself that's surprising, it's the fact that she sent it, her complete lack of self-awareness. Did she really expect a compliment? She didn't even take the care to tidy up the room, or to crop the photo, or to use a filter to eliminate the greasy glow on her face. Knut made just one critical remark to her after he received it. Actually, it was a question: *"Are you happy with this?"* No one is ever absolutely happy, she replied. *"Don't you think you've become a disaster psychologically, more than anything?"* he insisted. M. was hurt by his question. She asked him what he meant. He was referring to her shifting moods and how she often changed her mind, he said. *That's being a disaster?* M. asked. Of course, someone who is a disaster is psychologically confused.

She said: *"My cyclothymia is proof that I'm alive."* He replied: *"No. You're able to identify your cyclothymia because you're alive; and you could also do something about it and you'd still be alive."* *"You don't know me well enough to judge me like that,"* she said. *"Of course, now you'll start arguing with clichés: no one can know anybody, human beings are impenetrable, we understand but a glimmer of the human soul, time erases everything . . ."* he responded. He admits he was excessively abrasive with her, but he had been feeling tense about a phone number that was written in his notebook and he hadn't been able to identify. *You know how much forgetting something upsets me. I wrote the phone number, but I didn't know when, or whose it was, or why I wrote it down. I was trying to remember as I chatted with M., which made me even rougher with her.*

Sonia condemns his behavior. His attitude toward that woman is borderline cruel. Is it really necessary to treat her like that? Yes, he thinks it is. Her fickleness isn't limited to changing her mind, it's also a problem because she doesn't notice that she does it. That's why it's important that he points out her contradictions. Why does it matter that she contradicts herself?

Sonia asks him. Why does he care? *That's the other trap of fickleness: it makes us believe "it isn't a big deal" when in reality it matters, because fickleness reproduces by metastasis. Do you ever see your future self in M.? She may have been as good-looking as you, or even better looking, but now she can't hide the weight of time, which is not the same as its passing. I'm only trying to reflect on it, since neither of you is willing to do it.*

Willing to do what? Sonia answers. Reflect about what? He's always beating around the bush. Doesn't he realize how exhausting it is? *M. accuses me of the same thing. But it's really both of you who go round and round. My behavior is always straightforward: my actions represent a hard line, as is appropriate to the masculine symbolism.* And what is the feminine symbolism? Sonia asks. *The circle, obviously, where you both are trapped.*

M. and Sonia, Sonia and M.

One day Knut reveals another fantasy to Sonia. He could *do it* with M. while she lies next to them, so he can feel like he's *doing it* with Sonia. *You know I respect you too much to do it with you, but I do think it would be possible with an intermediary.* It wouldn't be as cold a scenario as it may seem. They could compensate for the lack of physical contact with looks and affectionate speech. For example, when M. went to the bathroom, he'd whisper something sweet in Sonia's ear, which would bring them close and exclude M. completely. *I could tell you that I love you, for example. Would that bother you?*

When Sonia reads this, she feels a knot of worry in her stomach. Until then it had all happened in the realm of fiction. Now, she realizes, Knut is trying to actualize the fantasies. Sonia is aware she's to blame. She didn't even like kissing him. What did she get herself into? It was she who, with that *I'm-not-sure-why* attitude he criticizes so much, encouraged him up to this point: it's she who fakes enthusiasm, who sent him pictures wearing the lingerie and the shoes, who suggested they meet, and who set the date when she knew it was all fake. She feels blocked, furious with herself, also slightly disgusted.

Why don't you write me back? he reproaches. *You make me feel awful. You see how far you can take your whims? You ask me to tell you my fantasies to immediately get scared. You call me out for being a prude when I don't write specific words, but you get startled and run away at the slightest discomfort.* She tells him her silence has nothing to do with what he wrote. No, she didn't get scared, she assures him. *It's just that right now I'm dealing with another issue. Something that prevents me from responding. I'll tell you as soon as I can. Give me a few days.*

It's precisely the amount of time she needs to think, although the hint of a possible solution, a believable way to escape the trap, has begun to effervesce in her mind.

The excuse is yet another fiction. Lies on top of lies. Who cares at this point? Verdú can still be useful to her for this. She tells Knut he found the last unopened package in the closet. She had left it there in a rush and didn't think Verdú would be curious about it, but he was. The worse part was her embarrassment—not having an answer prepared—how her lips started shaking, her red cheeks, the words that wouldn't quite come out, the babbling. The lingerie still had the price tags. Does Knut remember them? The garter, 215 euro; the two panties, 89 and 119 respectively; the bra, 185; the three pairs of panty hose: 40, 45, and 45. To make it all the more confusing, the package had creams, a bunch of mechanical pencils, a drawing compass, a new cell-phone case, a nail clipper, and a few little boxes of dried saffron. Not to mention the addresses on the box. To: her, From: him. How could she explain all of that?

She first told Verdú she had done some online shopping. *"You paid that much for underwear? Are you crazy?"* she says he asked. No, no it was a lot cheaper, she told him. She just felt like treating herself. He didn't believe her. He pressured her until Sonia caved and admitted that they were gifts. *"Gifts from whom?"* she tells Knut that Verdú asked. From a friend. *"What kind of friend gives you those gifts?"* She told him she had a friend who worked at La Perla and got a great discount on the lingerie. *"What about the Armani panty hose, and the Dior creams? And the rest of the things? Where did they come from? Come on, Sonia,"* she says Verdú told her, *"That's absurd. I've never even seen you wear anything remotely similar."* The funny thing is, Sonia tells Knut, the explanation she gave him was not far from the truth: weren't they gifts from a friend after all? *But he didn't believe me.*

Verdú left the house for a couple of days without telling her where he was staying. *When he gets angry at me, that's what he usually does, he avoids confrontation. He pushes me away by leaving me alone and I don't know what to do to appease him.* She called his cell phone quite a few times but it went straight to voicemail. He wouldn't answer her texts either. On the third night, when she was finally able to sleep, she caught a glimpse of him taking a clean shirt from the closet—in reality, the closet hasn't had any of Verdú's shirts in it for a long time. Sonia took the opportunity to beg him to come back, to explain everything and apologize.

Everything? Knut asks. Well, not *Eh-verything*, but something close, a sanitized version. She didn't tell him about the previous gifts, for example. She made him think it was the first time she had received something from him. She didn't tell him that she had known Knut for years, even before meeting him, or that, other than the lapse when they got married, they'd been writing to each other ever since. She didn't say she emails him her stories and he helps her improve them. And, of course, she didn't say a word of their plans to see each other in Cárdenas, or that they had met there once before. *Well that sure is a sanitized version . . .* Knut says. Did he forgive her? Yes, she thinks so. But he made her promise she would never receive gifts from him again; and it gets worse: he asked her to promise she would cut contact with him immediately. She had to agree to it. *I didn't have a choice, please understand*, she asks him.

Knut had never shown so much fear of losing her, not even the first time they parted ways. This time, like in previous arguments they'd had, disappointment and rage were most prominent: but before, it was each of their hurt prides confronting the other's. *Now we're dependent on the imposition of a third person, which genuinely terrifies me.*

He's horrified by the prospect of never seeing her again. Is it really that impossible for her to come to Cárdenas without Verdú finding out? Could she come and leave the same day and say it's for work like she did last time? Does she think that's viable? It wouldn't even be about trying to do anything with her anymore if he could only see her; he just wants to see her. He'd be content with very little: to maybe just contemplate her with a pair of stockings or a bra, like on that perfect day they lived together. Losing all the other options doesn't matter to him. *I'm even happy that these obstacles have come to be. There's nothing more pleasurable in a fantasy than knowing it's impossible to realize.* But losing it all is too much.

She tells him not to insist. She reminds him she shouldn't even be writing to him. Whenever she mentions this possibility, not writing to him ever again, Knut becomes desperate, he begs her to keep in contact, to not give up, to not throw away such a special relationship, one they've nurtured for so many years, just because she's being pressured by someone who can't understand—and will never understand—what they have. He gradually gives up his aspirations: okay, he won't see her, he won't send her any more gifts, but can they at least still write each other now and then? They can keep it strictly within the literary realm. *We can talk about books. You can keep sending me what you write and we can discuss it. Whatever happens, you should never stop writing!* What would be the problem if they stay within the bounds of literature? Not even the most jealous of husbands could be bothered by that sort of relationship. She could even keep receiving books. What's wrong with that? *If you notice, God wanted the package that Verdú found to not have any books. If he sees you come home with new titles, it's unlikely that he'll suspect anything. He probably thinks I'm a pervert, someone who just wants to f . . . his wife and can't realize I am your most fervent admirer . . . literary admirer. But that is the truth. There won't be anyone like me. I'm just asking you to not rush your decision, to think about it.*

10. BUS RIDE

PASSENGERS GET ON and off at each stop. An accidental shove, an elbow, an *excuse me, pardon me.* Sonia gives her seat to an elderly man. Her thoughts race the entire ride. *To keep going,* to continue no matter what. A never-ending spiral. Holes, needs, yearnings. Words, price tags, boxes. New passengers get on. Everything is always excessive. It keeps expanding, filtering through, slipping in through the thinnest of cracks. The bus shakes, someone complains. He wants to be everywhere. In what she reads. In what she writes. In what she wears. In what she thinks. The pretenses. The fake submissiveness, the fake acceptance, the fake love. The elderly man gets off the bus, Sonia gets her seat back. Pretending to read, pretending to write, pretending to wear something, pretending to think a certain way. Pretending Verdú is there, pretending she wants to see him. Pretending to be a soul mate. Pretending to be a mother. Pretending to be a daughter. Pretending to be a sister. Pretending to be surprised. Pretending to be upset.

A light drizzle stains the windows.

A pair of shoes in a half-empty closet. That she doesn't want to wear. That she can't give away. That she can't sell. That she doesn't want to throw away. That she wants to return.

The raindrops begin to slide sideways on the glass.

They're gorgeous, Knut says. Cream colored with a T-strap that has silver studs. *You'll love them. They're the last ones. They're very special to me.* No. She won't love them. She's always hated that color in shoes. Silver studs? Not her style at all. She could care less about brand names.

She told him. She warned him. And now they're in her closet.

The reproach: *you're not even going to wait to try them on?* The accusation: *you're so ungrateful.* The question: *what do you have to lose?* The argument: *I took them for you and I'm going to send them.*

The bus empties and fills again and again, like a breathing lung that swells and shrinks, and always remains. *To keep going.* The years go by so quickly.

The blue hue of the light shining on the shoes. The hint of sweat in her armpits. A moral recovery, he called them. There's so much beauty in those images.

Do you know what Proust said about lying?

He read it that morning. And it's beautiful. And it's true.

Lying is essential because the truth can't be communicated.

The rain becomes intense. She'd have a drink or two right now.

She can't, she tells herself.

But she can. Of course she can.

11. THREE MONTHS BEFORE

War is really this,
but at a different scale.

SHE HEARS PANTING behind the gate, constricted breathing from the pressure of a leash, the beginning of a drowned-out bark, full of anguish, when the neighbor's dog recognizes her. She smiles when she finally sees it, comes close to pet its head. The neighbor says something under her breath. A hello, is Sonia's best guess.

He's a big boy, huh? He must need to run around a lot, doesn't he? Sonia says, still smiling.

The woman answers in a dry tone.

No. Everyone thinks that. But the larger breeds are calm. Dog lovers know that the nervous breeds are the medium ones, not the large ones.

Ah, I see. Sonia says. She squats and puts the cardboard box on the floor to start talking to the animal.

Hey, handsome. Yeah, you're a handsome boy. You know who I am, don't you? I see you in the courtyard all the time.

The neighbor yanks the leash away. The dog starts to trot behind her, wagging his tail and sniffing around. They come out to the street. Sonia is still squatting. She eventually gets up, confused. Did her neighbor get upset? She left so abruptly, without even saying goodbye.

She picks up the box, and carries it against her waist while she climbs up the stairs and opens her door. She puts it on the table next to her laptop, the open books, the drafts of stories she hasn't finished. *You're never going to write again are you?* the insidious accusation persists. Sonia gives Knut evasive answers each time he asks. She sometimes cites her tiredness, others her lack of confidence, and almost always her lack of free time. She has a family and a job, she says: does he really think she has any energy left to write?

You see how you contradict yourself? Not too long ago you criticized my view of employment as slavery and now you admit that it's the main reason preventing you from writing, but you get mad at me if I point out how impulsive you are in your comments. I'd like to picture you at your job, surrounded by hardworking people like you, proud of their contributions, bursting with generosity as they give themselves entirely to the task of writing reports, with the kind of motivation Luther had when he studied the Bible . . . but then I realize it's a ridiculous image. I'd like to think your coworkers reflect about Hitler, about world hunger, about Bach . . . but take a look at them . . . They probably don't even remember their own childhoods, do they? They've probably never repented before God. If the great flood came tomorrow they'd be the first ones to be dragged away by the waves. What are you doing there? Why don't you let me help you escape? You didn't even ask if they would cut your hours, like we talked about. You don't let me send you anything anymore. You stupidly spend the money you earn even more stupidly. But I won't get tired of telling you: you'll be able to justify your existence in the future only if you write.

Sonia looks at the package on the table. The label with her name written on it. The same neatness as always. The firm strokes that form the shapes of the letters in all caps. Straight, hard lines. Masculine symbolism, as he says. She thinks about the dog. The upset neighbor. She scratches the edges of the box. Her anxiety starts to set in, it spreads little by little. Books. Just like in the beginning. Only books. How did she end up in the same situation? *Let's try to get you out of that place safe and sound.* His words resound in her mind. She knows exactly what he means. She feels as though Knut had made plans for her even before knowing about her, or sensing her existence.

He hasn't stopped insisting on it in the last few weeks: since the shipments didn't work, what about giving her money so she can write exclusively? How much would she need a month? Maybe he can get it. *Can you imagine?* he asks her. *You quit your job and write in the mornings while your son is at school. Hours and hours for yourself. To read, and write, and proof. For us to be in touch more often, with the sole goal of supporting you.*

There's no point in reasoning with him, in trying to make him see it's a failed idea, an impossible feat, or that she simply doesn't want it. She tells him she has many expenses. The mortgage, the bills, her son. *But Verdú's income covers part of it, right?* Yes, she agrees immediately, because it's true after all. *I can contribute the rest. You should trust more in my liquidity. What makes you think I don't have plenty to spend?* As proof, he tells her he gave M. a thousand euro recently, just like that. *You can't say I treat her so badly now, can you?* M. asked him for five hundred the other day. *This is another one of her contradictions, like I tell you. She's always pretending to bathe in abundance, appearing to be in close contact with friends in high society, she mentions often she has exquisite taste and how certain things are beneath her, but the first time we met she suggested a 40-euro room in an inn and now she asks me for 500 euro out of the blue. She just said she needed them and couldn't say for what. Not only that, she said she wasn't sure when she would pay them back. I gave her a thousand and told her she owes me nothing. She was very happy.*

His spending habits aren't conservative either. He just started a facial hair removal treatment for example. The dermatologist recommended a state-of-the-art laser technique without side effects, recently imported from the United States. It's the best, and also the most expensive, but the price doesn't deter him. He even plans to treat his chest and back. He's always cared about looks, she knows this. When he's finished with those treatments he'll fix his teeth as well. A root canal, a couple of bridges, and whitening: he'll, of course, have work done on anything he can.

So you have enough money to lend to your friend, for laser hair removal and cosmetic dentistry, and you'll also have enough to send me every month . . . I'm sorry, but I don't believe you. He argues so convincingly that for brief moments Sonia believes him. She thinks maybe she's been ignoring the fact that there are parts of Knut's life she knows nothing about. Maybe his family is rich, she tells herself, but immediately remembers the picture of the skirt spread out on the bed he sent, and the neighborhood he lives in. She'd visited his street on Google Maps before: tall brick blocks with very narrow yards and fences covered in graffiti. What if he makes money from other kinds of business deals? Whichever way he gets it, does no one in his home notice? Do his parents think it's normal that he doesn't have a job but dresses in expensive clothes? That he goes to sleep at odd times and accumulates books? That he can pay for laser hair removal? She worked up the courage to ask him a few times. *No, they don't say anything,* he would answer. OR: *They don't pay attention.* OR: *You habitually think anything that doesn't match your reality is abnormal, don't you? Why should they think anything of it?* He would think it much stranger if his daughter, after having studied for years and years, now spent more and more years locked in an office building that doesn't pay her enough, or leave enough time for her to do what she really likes. *Or do you think that what you do is normal just because you do it? And that nothing you do could ever be abnormal? Life can't be judged by those parameters. No, what I do isn't normal, but I could care less. Artistic creation is born from abnormality.*

And, of course he's being serious. Has she never heard of sponsorship? Of course she has, Sonia says, but it doesn't work that way. *Oh no? Does sponsorship always have to be institutional? Have there been no private patrons in history? They haven't been few, that's for sure . . . Don't you know James Joyce and Ezra Pound's story?* The real issue is that she doesn't trust him. If a state department or a foundation offered her a grant she'd not only take it happily, she'd brag about it everywhere. What's the difference with his proposition? Only that he's the sponsor? The guarantees are the same. Actually, there are even more benefits.

But we fight all the time! she says. *How will I know that you won't quit on me?* Knut reminds her that when they fight it's always after she initiates it, she's the one who wants to end the relationship, who refuses to write to him or continue to receive his help. *Never have I ever, not even in the worst fights, wanted to separate from you.* Sonia admits this is true, but still, she tells him, she doesn't want to owe him anything. Plus, what would Verdú think of that arrangement? Does Knut think he wouldn't suspect it's him? Knut has answers for that too. No, he has no reason to suspect anything if she tells him it's a grant from a writing program or from the arts and culture state department, or whatever she wants. *And you won't owe me anything. There will be no charges, no bills. This isn't a favor I want to do for you. This is simply a way to be true to my own convictions, and to whom I've been in your life all this time.*

And then what? Does he think because she writes for a year or two her life will be perfect? That she'll be able to return to work whenever she pleases? Things aren't as easy as he thinks. If she leaves her job, they won't be waiting with open arms for her to return. But Knut's convinced that once her writing takes off, she'll never need an office job again. Her writing is good enough—and commercial enough—for her to live off the profits eventually. Until that happens, she'll have him. However many years it takes. If it makes her feel more at ease, they can sign a contract. An annual, renewable contract for one thousand euro a month. Signed by a notary and with all the necessary provisions. What does she think? And no, he's not proposing it because he holds fantastical views. *It's the opposite: with God as my witness, I have complete certainty that you can do it. I've had it ever since I've known you. For fu . . . 's sake! Why would I do it if I didn't?*

Day after day is spent going over both sides of the same argument. Sonia is exhausted. She threatens not to write again if he doesn't let it go. It is what it is. Take it or leave it. *See? You always get your way in the end,* he reproaches. More disappointed than sad, more confused than angry, he claims not to understand her attitude. *I understand your refusal to receive any more gifts, aside from books, because of that Bluebeard specimen that lives with you, but your rejection of this offer truly baffles me.* He asks her to give him a reason, just one reason. *I've given you thousands!* she says. No. Those were just excuses. Not one of them is a valid reason for her refusal. Sonia warns him, she's not going to argue about this anymore. Not one more word on the subject, she insists. And since he continues, she's silent. *When you're slightly offended you display a great deal of righteousness; when you're offended in moderate measure, you try to offend back; and when you're very offended, you usually become silent. That's how you work. I can't understand why you don't want to discuss the issue. It's just no, and no, and more no.* What's the point of having a discussion? It's as if Sonia's hermetically sealed. She's against anything he proposes. *It's because you think it hurts your ego, but you should take into consideration that the ego doesn't exist. When we argue, it's not you and I concretely who are having the argument.* Letting a fight affect them only makes sense if life were eternal, but I doesn't exist. What exists is a universal will into which individuals are dissolved. That's why she shouldn't be offended by anything. Offenses are just another illusion of the I. *The day you understand all this, it will be too late and you'll have let this opportunity go by. Just like you always do with me: you let everything drift away.*

Can I ask you one last favor? Of course, Sonia replies. *Would you accept a pair of shoes?* She can't believe it: again? Knut sends her a link so she can see them: cream-colored, high-heel shoes with a T-strap that has silver studs. From a limited-edition collection. Armani. 385 euro. Sonia finds them hideous but she keeps her opinion to herself. She does remind him that they agreed he would send only books. *You promised we wouldn't stray from the strictly literary, didn't you?* This is different, he says. First of all, it isn't clear whether footwear—at the very least this kind of shoe—doesn't belong in the literary realm. Has she looked at them closely? A quick glance isn't enough. If she takes note of the details, she'll see they're a splendid pair of shoes. *But we won't ponder conceptually what's literary and what isn't.* Secondly, he's already told her that this represents a favor. Asking someone for a favor implies that the person being asked steps out of their comfort zone. The person who does someone a favor gives something up to do it. In this case, she would renounce— although just this once—her decision to receive only books. *If it didn't represent a break from the agreement, it wouldn't be a favor, you would just be going along with it . . . I would just send them to you, I wouldn't even ask for your permission.* Since she shows resistance he changes his argumentative tone to a supplicant one. *If I've meant anything to you, if you've ever felt the smallest appreciation for me, I beg you to accept them. You refused out of pride to receive what I wanted to give you most. This is much smaller. It's the only favor I will ask you until I die. You have no idea what it means to me.*

He tells her he got them on an afternoon while he was out with M. *I'd spent all day grabbing things for her, another proof that my behavior toward her isn't as severe as you perceive.* All sorts of products, anything M. felt like getting. Except lingerie, he clarifies. *I could do that only with you.* It didn't take him too long to get them. Deactivating the alarm when the clerk went to the back room took a couple of minutes. He then put one in his jacket pocket and the other in his shopping bag. And voila. M. thought they were for her at first. No, he told her. Can't she see they're not her size? Whom were they for then? She looked at them intently with her watery eyes. The corners of her mouth were covered in crumbs from a pastry she'd just devoured. For a friend. *"Your friend's very lucky,"* she said. *I pointed out I had snagged a lot of presents for her too, but human beings are like this: we never have enough.*

He plopped himself on the bed in the hotel room and held up one of the shoes to look at it. He must've spent more than an hour doing that: putting it down, picking it up, putting it down, picking it up. M. didn't say anything. She just kept smoking and covering the comforter with cigarette ash. She later lay down and went to sleep. Knut took much longer to fall asleep. A heavy rain hit the window. He tried to concentrate on the sound of the rain to tune out M.'s snoring: it took so much effort that he got a headache, and the exhaustion from it eventually put him to sleep. He woke up before M. The shoes were on the floor next to him. He picked one up and held it against the blue light of the new day. The sky was clear after the rain. He pictured the shoe on Sonia's foot and thought she was the only one who could pull off high heels like those. *I imagined your wonderful legs wrapped in a pair of shining sheer stockings. I got extremely aroused and did it to M.; I cut right to the chase while she was still sleeping, pretending her body was yours.*

These are possibly the most stimulating shoes he's ever taken. *If I send them to your office, Verdú doesn't have to find out.* He asks Sonia to take them home one day when he's not around and take a picture with them. Only her legs. Just wearing stockings and those shoes. *Although if you feel like it, since I won't see you ever again, you could raise the camera and photograph yourself from the waist down . . . Naked, just the stockings and the shoes. Could you do that for me? Don't you think I've earned it after all these years?*

She opens the box and holds one of the shoes up, it could be the
same one he held in the hotel room. The package also has some
books she doesn't bother looking at. The shoe smells like new
leather. It's rigid, flashy, and very heavy. She puts it back in the
box and kicks the box to the back of the closet. She runs out the
door to catch the bus.

Racing thoughts and memories of words crowd her mind
during the entire bus ride.

A pair of shoes in a half-empty closet. That she doesn't want
to wear. That she can't give away. That she can't sell. That she
doesn't want to throw away. That she wants to return.

It starts to pour outside. The raindrops slide sideways on the
glass.

She can't, no, she tells herself. But she can. Of course she
can. Holding on to the handlebar above, moved around by
the shoves of people getting on and off, she suddenly feels
the weight of determination. When she arrives at her office,
the first thing she does is write to Knut. She does it enraged,
brimming with resentment. She knows that if she lets this
one go, in a few days another pair of shoes will arrive, then
perfumes, creams, lingerie, and they'll start all over again. She's
fed up: her colorless, flavorless, neutral passivity has become a
thick, reeking substance. She wants to say it like that but she
isn't trying to make literature. She simply tells him she thinks
the shoes are horrendous. That she doesn't care anymore about
keeping or not keeping the agreement: they're just horrendous
and she doesn't want them. If they were at least pretty, but they
aren't. She enjoys repeating the term: *horrendous*. She warned
him not to send them, but he's stubborn and deaf, and didn't
bother finding out the reason. Now she's going to have to send
them back. *Let's see if you get it this time.* A picture wearing them
he says? From the waist down, wearing stockings and the shoes
only? There it is: nothing he gives her is free, he's always wanted

to get his prize. She's tired of being a pawn in his demented projects. *Sick and tired,* she says. *You're demented,* she repeats. She's never spoken so harshly to him.

The reply arrives within a few minutes. *Oh please. I didn't send you a box full of putrid jellyfish, did I? What's the reason for your anger? That I gave you a pair of shoes you don't like? I haven't threatened your life, or insulted, or mistreated you, or done anything for you to get like that.*

He will say, it hurts him that she questions the intentions behind his gifts. Did she think they walked a lot when she visited him in Cárdenas? Well, she should multiply that by ten, and then the weight of the bags by five to begin to understand how he spends his afternoons. *Leaving the house, searching a mall, not finding a book there, going to another one, not finding it there either, heading to the supermarket, putting the things I snagged in a train-station locker, going to another mall, heading back to the lockers, going to the next mall, leaving a few other items in a recycling container, coming back, picking everything up . . .* Not to mention the possible inconveniences that come with the risk of being caught. He's strictly illustrating the energy the process requires. It also involves taking the items to his house or someone else's, negotiating timelines with them, coming back to get the items, snagging mailing tape, finding a box, spending the night preparing the box, getting up early to get it to the post office . . . *That's a lot of work to get a picture, given that there are infinitely more exciting ones available absolutely everywhere, don't you think? Do you really believe I lack that much self-awareness? Since this isn't something I do for anyone else, let's focus on my relationship with you, shall we? Beyond the picture, which you indeed could choose to send me or not, and it wouldn't change my feelings toward you. If I were looking for "that" exclusively, I wouldn't have had to pursue you for years. Call me extravagant, exaggerated, crazy if it pleases you, but, for God's sake, don't treat me like an idiot!*

He asks her to think about her closest girlfriend. Can she picture her going to get the seventeen books for her Italian classes that she asked him for? What about the strainers, the kitchen scissors, the valerian root supplements? He's not proposing a hypothesis where her friend steals these items and gives them to her, but one where she simply makes the trips he makes to go get them, with Sonia's own money in her pockets if she likes. *She'd be sick of it by the third store and tell you to just get it all online.*

How pathetic, that she's spent several years—not days, or weeks, or a couple of months, but nothing short of several years—devoted to someone as worthless as him. *It has to be a hard pill for you to swallow, with all the others you could've met. And for what in the end? For this. For nothing.*

Sonia keeps her word and sends him back the shoes. She plans to stop talking to him as well. Whatever he says, she won't let him provoke her and she won't be softened or fall for his begging either. What she didn't expect was his reaction when he got the shoes. Knut accuses her of returning the shoes in *terrible* shape. The soles have wear marks from her walking in them. The logo isn't visible in one because of the scratches. He tried using a repair cream but it didn't work. Has she really not worn them? Or is she returning them in that state to somehow come out on top? What is he supposed to do with them like this? He can't even sell them or give them to another woman. When Sonia tells him she doesn't believe him, he sends pictures so she can see the damage. *Being the way you are, I am sure you think I'm exaggerating, but the pictures speak for themselves.* Yes, he is exaggerating, she says. The pictures barely show some faint marks, probably from other women trying the shoes on at the store. She hasn't taken a single step in them, she can assure him. *You're neurotic. And an insufferable perfectionist*, she tells him.

Knut admits it. *And a fetishist*, he adds. *Even after I told you how important these shoes were, you do this to me. You know perfectly well that by damaging the shoes you're hurting me. It doesn't surprise me that you would want to send a message through the shoes, to tell me how disgusted you are by me now. It's the natural reaction of someone like you, who always wants to come out on top.*

Sonia makes a conscious effort not to reply, but he keeps writing. *It still pains me to look at those shoes but I know I'll have to do something with them eventually. I find your silence fitting. What good can I expect from you? None, because you act entirely on whim, you're selfish, lazy, vindictive, and much worse. But I'll be here, whether you like it or not, whether you read this or not.* He tells her about his latest expeditions—*to obtain horrendous things of course*—about his trips to the laser hair removal clinic, about his altercations with the nurses and with M. He also sends her pictures of decrepit old men, and fragments of news articles about scientific discoveries that she has no idea how to interpret. He read a theory about arthropods in a magazine—*the most primitive beings currently living on earth, as you know*—in which the reason for their survival of every major environmental catastrophe is thought to be precisely that they've hardly evolved. *The equivalent of such an elementary degree of evolutionary development in human beings would be our moral indifference—an issue with tragic implications according to Proust. It's obvious that you're a particularly sensitive young woman. It amazes me how you head nowhere without any concern.*

After another dose of silence, calm finally seems to set in. A heavyhearted calm that doesn't quite satisfy Sonia, who opens the closet to look at the remains of the battle. Bags pile up in her closet. Scattered and bunched-up clothes mixed together everywhere, they've become old before ever being worn. Knut's right. She's messy and lazy, and that lack of care reveals an ambiguous contempt. Disgust, is how he put it. She organizes what she can still sell or give away. She throws out the rest without feeling sorry this time. She sees her neighbors moving boxes when she takes the clothes out to the garbage containers. They're loading an old moving van rather quickly, carrying suitcases, unassembled furniture, a giant, not-so-clean mattress. They seem to be doing it angrily. Where's the dog? she wonders. She constantly checks the courtyard during the next few days, overcoming the temptation to drink, over and over again. Silence all around. The dog is obviously gone. Did they give him away? Or worse, did they abandon him?

One morning, shortly before six, her landline phone rings. Sonia picks up sleepily. Before she gets a chance to be surprised or frightened, Knut's voice screams on the other side. His desperate yelling drags her into the confused state of someone who can't or won't understand what is happening to them. *What is it?* she says groggy, even though Knut is telling her. His explanation is so convoluted and dark—a mix of rage, pain, bewilderment, and hate—that it takes her some time to understand what he's saying.

She looks at one of the walls in her bedroom—notices the outline of a square shape, lighter than the rest of the wall, left by a frame that used to hang over it—and listens, speechless.

It wasn't improbable, yet she didn't stop and think it could happen. Her lack of foresight, he says. Her impulsivity, that malicious spontaneity. Her irrational nature, he says. He just wants to know the reason. *Why?* he asks her, *Why?* What sort of dark impulse, what evil mechanism within her motivated her to do this to him? To him, who's spent the last years of his life living for her, who's watched over her every step. To him, who loved her, who truly loved her, who cared about her like he hasn't cared about anyone, and now finds out the kind of monster that lives inside of her. *This is like* Scarlet Street, *when the spell of Edward G. Robinson's fascination breaks . . .* He'll tell her later this morning in an email, and he'll keep demanding an explanation.

Sonia doesn't know how to answer. She lacks an explanation.

12. BOOK

I'D BE LYING if I said I was surprised when I heard the news. I knew it would happen sooner or later. Of course I would like you to send me the book. Remember to send it to the new address at the end of this note. I now live in the same street as the building where you tried on that shirt almost four years ago. I assume you remember. It's hard to know with you. You're so proud of being forgetful!

When you send me the book, could you write a dedication? "To my best reader," or "To my only reader," or "To my reader," or all of it, "To my best and only reader, my reader." Don't I deserve the gesture?

Do you want my opinion? My honest opinion?

To answer your question, I'm doing well. Enough time has passed for me to realize and accept that I'm not the kind of man, or person, that you tend to like. Don't think I haven't realized the reverse as well, I have. It was most obvious with the clothes. When I would send you stockings, shirts, lingerie, shoes, gloves, scarves, and jackets nonstop, I was dressing a character. You would discreetly tell me it wasn't your style but my stubbornness knew no limits. I was so intent on perceiving you according to my imagination that I was blind to reality. In that respect, you sure tolerated a lot from me; because if someone, even someone I liked very much, started to buy me jeans and t-shirts and sneakers or wanted me to grow a beard, I would find it extremely irritating.

What happened with the rest of the shoes and lingerie? All the things you told me you'd keep? I don't really care if you donated it all or threw it away. I truly mean it. As it turns out, what I'm really grateful for, and I will be my entire life, is the eBay scheme. It's the most valuable lesson I learned from you. I just wish I'd thought of it before. It was an excellent idea on your part. As for me, I don't think I'll ever snag any lingerie or clothes again. It's boring to me now just to think back to one of those afternoons cruising malls for hours, looking for what I thought you would like or what you'd ask me for . . .

You're not with anyone now, are you? You speak about your breakup with Verdú with odd detachment. I confess that I always suspected you had broken up long before and didn't tell me. Toward the end you barely mentioned him, except as an excuse to limit our relationship. One day, a few months before I found out about your betrayal, I called your house and your son picked up. I didn't expect to hear a child's voice. You may have been in the shower, who knows. I must've been suspecting it for a long time by then because I spontaneously asked to speak with his "dad." "He doesn't live here," he answered. I didn't ask you about it out of respect.

I do still see M. now and then. She mostly calls me when she needs money. Everything that was germinating in her has fully manifested. I see other women as well. The number grows constantly, believe it or not.

Just out of curiosity: will you be coming to Cárdenas for the book presentation? Or for interviews, or one of those book clubs that people like now? Don't worry, I'm not asking so I can see you. I wouldn't even try to see you from a distance. Although if you wanted . . .

Will you run with the little literary circles? I picture you mingling with those types quite gracefully. They'll praise you, there's no doubt about it. There will be more than a few people who will try to get close to you through flattery and flirt with you. And you won't even remember that I was the first to point out your talent.

My advice is to stay away from all pretense and fakeness from the very beginning. Can you imagine Joyce or Kafka mingling at a book club?

I don't want to give you the impression that I am mad at you. I know I might have when I answered your text so abrasively yesterday. I was just leaving the gym and had found out I lost 4,000 euro in stocks (it's true). It was extremely cloudy outside too; that always gives me a headache. I also have a trial in two days (go ahead, laugh) for snagging three CDs. In normal psychological conditions, I wouldn't have written a phrase like, "as far as the news and your reappearance is concerned," not even because of the immediacy of using my cell phone. I'm tormented by mistakes like that. I haven't changed in that regard.

There—is—something I'd like you to understand. Although it would be best if you did without my influence. My excessiveness was not good, but your laxity wasn't either. Both come close to what can be labeled as "mental issues." That said, I not only think of myself as a good person, I think of myself as a very good person, a much better person than you could even imagine. If I weren't, I wouldn't have dedicated my entire life to theft or spent so many years treating you to generous gifts. My excessiveness can lead to an almost Calderonian honor, but if events don't turn out the way I expect them to, my ego isn't hurt by admitting defeat . . .

You didn't even send me the empty perfume bottles I asked you for, and you promised you'd save them. You couldn't even do that. But even if you didn't, I suppose I still love you.

13. THREE YEARS BEFORE

Whenever I think of us, the same
phrase always comes to mind:
"Once in a lifetime." And no, I'm not
satisfied by the simplest answer.
The expression has been with me
far too long. It has to mean something.
I imagine it follows the same logic
as mistakes or unconscious forgetting.

SONIA PICTURES IT vividly. She sees it and she can feel, in part, a sliver of his pain; but discomfort overshadows any other feeling she could be having. She knows what she's done is wrong, but she asks herself: what could she have done? did she actually have other options? was it wrong of her to do it? or was the wrongdoing in her poor planning? She shakes her head. There's no use in pondering those questions now, she tells herself.

She imagines Knut in front of his computer, visiting eBay for the first time in his life. The darkness of the room, the greenish light from the laptop shining on his face. His impatient expression, the marks on his skin giving away his habitual nervous tension. He kept the shoes in his room—carefully wrapped, unlike she did—until he was able to better remove the scratches on the soles. This entailed numerous trips to shoe stores to ask which repair creams were the best, and many others to shopping centers in order to *obtain* them. Altogether it had been many days of work. He relied on his usual patience and tenacity. He then waited for the cream to work on the leather. He reapplied it once again. He took long looks at the shoes that had represented so much promise—fantasy, freedom, beauty—and were now just expensive shoes destined to belong to a woman somewhere far away, whom he didn't feel like dreaming of. He photographed them on a piece of dark-colored cardboard from various angles. He uploaded the images to his computer and edited them to add sharpness. He wanted the details and the good craftsmanship to show. The stitches, the studs, the shiny T-strap, the strap buckles, everything that Sonia showed disdain for. He surfed eBay with a knot in his stomach. He didn't feel like doing it, but he approached the task with the same seriousness he does everything in his life. He wondered for how much he could sell a pair of Armani shoes without the box and some, still, lightly visible scratches. He figured he should check what other users do. Do other people sell designer shoes there? He searches, and yes, he finds quite a few. All sold. Very cheap. Knockoffs? Originals? Impossible to tell without a closer look. He clicks on each ad and zooms in on the pictures, still feeling skeptical. What a coincidence he thinks. He stretches his legs, focuses again on the screen, coming a bit closer. Similar model, same size. A lighthearted description written in an upbeat tone. *Want to take home a pair of original Armani shoes for a ridiculously low price? These heels will make the guys curious and the girls jealous. They can be yours for only 40 euro.* The seller— the username is immediately recognizable—has been offering other Armani shoes and many more items for some time. To Knut, the images seem to be falling over him, as heavy as stones. One after another, ads for perfumes, gloves, scarves, stockings, dilapidating him in the midst of confusion. Even though the ads have Sonia's name written all over them, it takes him some time to understand it, and much longer to admit it. He feels dizzy, he can't quite process the facts. He keeps clicking on each ad, reading the descriptions, completely fascinated. He's absolutely sure at this point but he feels compelled to continue looking at the same time, he can't stop himself.

I still can't remember the exact moment I became aware of your betrayal, he tells her. *It was all so confusing, so . . . nebulous. It's funny, in that moment what hurt the most were the compliments you got from buyers in the reviews. All those people saying "Sonia's great . . ." and ". . . it's a pleasure doing business with her." All of a sudden it seemed like the Sonia they were writing about was a stranger to me, someone completely outside of my reality. That was the biggest lie.*

Too much pain. Too much shock. He got in bed and covered his head with the comforter to drown out his crying. He got up after a while and went back to the computer to continue to look at the details in the ads. He wanted to call her immediately but he felt paralyzed in front of the screen. He spent forty-five minutes in the living room waiting for his cell phone to charge. He felt worse, and worse, and worse each minute that went by: to a point where he wasn't sure if he'd be able to bear it. He feared she would deny it, or that she'd hang up, or that she wouldn't even take the call. He was afraid he would hear a burst of laughter, or insults. *It was as if I had suddenly discovered I was in prison and you had decided my sentence.* At six in the morning he couldn't take it anymore. His hands were shaking. He felt a burning sensation inside. He got intense stomach cramps. He went to the bathroom two or three times. Finally he picked up the phone and called her.

She says she feels ashamed. She tells him she didn't mean to hurt him, that he needs to believe her. She didn't want him to feel rejected, she almost felt forced to do it, it was her only alternative to throwing it all away. Each time she insinuated to him that she didn't need anything else, or that the pieces he sent weren't her style, or that she had enough, or that she didn't have room for anything else, he refused to take her hints. He was stubborn beyond belief, she says. Yes, the choice she made wasn't the right one. She can see that now. She won't say she's sorry or ask him to forgive her because she knows she doesn't deserve it but, she tells him, if her intention was to make money, she wouldn't have asked him to stop sending her gifts, she would've encouraged him. Can't he see? Whatever the intention though, she realizes the damage has been done. How can she make it up to him? she asks.

They talk about money. He demands that she pay him whatever she got from those sales. Sonia isn't sure how much it is. She hasn't been keeping a record. It's been two years of sporadic, disorganized sales. Still, she calculates an approximate amount in an attempt to be fair. It comes out to a little over 1,000 euro for products whose original price probably totaled more than 6,000 euro. *You know what to do then,* he says. *I want a thousand euro in my account immediately.* Sonia takes money out of her savings and borrows the rest from a friend. She makes the deposit. But that isn't enough to put out the fire. The embers still give off heat inside Knut, burning him at times. He moves them every day, stoking them with sadness and pain. Sonia has to swallow them too. How could she do anything else?

She begs him not to dwell on the details. She disables her eBay account so he can't look through her history. But it's too late, Knut remembers perfectly what he saw. *Your ads, the way you expressed yourself in them,* he tells her. *The large, colorful font, the exclamation marks, the backgrounds with floral designs, that little flattering tone for the prospective buyer—like in outdated marketing campaigns—it all has a cheery fluidity I didn't know you possessed.* It would never in a million years occur to him to express himself that way, he says bitterly. It's not that he finds it wrong or right. It's that it shows a horrific degree of commitment to the endeavor. *There you were, coming up with sales pitches while you maintained the fiction of our correspondence. As much as I try, I can't accept that both of you are the same person:*

the one who wrote me, and the one who profited selling my gifts without telling me . . . Although it's true I had told you before about the duality I see in you.

He wouldn't even expect that kind of behavior from, say, the people who pressed the button on the gas chambers: so consistently cold and detached, so unconcerned.

Yes, he knows he shouldn't follow certain trains of thought but he can't help it. *I remember something I said to you in Cárdenas after we finished lunch, "I want to help you take care of your hands. I don't want them to ever be cold; I want you to be able to keep them pretty and polished." You confessed later that my comments moved you.* He then gave her the RoC creams and nail polish, in all sorts of colors: every one she asked for. He also gave her the pair of Tous gloves. *You had never owned leather gloves. You said you found them perfect, snuggly, warm, very comfortable, elegant. Now I see that you sold them.* And the jacket. That exquisite, expensive, white Armani jacket they both liked so much. She also sold it. She got rid of it for 49 euro. Which goes to show the extent of her duplicity. It would have been better if she at least gave it away, he tells her.

And the shirt. *It was a memento. You didn't care either? Did it take up so much room in your closet that you had to sell it for . . . 9 euro?* He remembers the scene every day. The light in the hallway enveloping them, subtle, yellow. The floating dust. The beauty against that sordid backdrop, beaming, daring, completely canceling out the filth he's so disgusted by. That silence: the buffered traffic noise in the distance. How she stretched her arms to change shirts, her tempting armpits. The curve of her breasts held by that lace bra with three fabrics in the cup, the shimmering silk. *There was also the scar, your ugly scar. I told you I saw it, and later regretted it. Now I realize how meaningful that sign was. None other than the confirmation of the reality I was so determined to disguise.*

If I hadn't met you, my life would've been more or less the same. I would've had this false and fictitious relationship with someone else, someone without your qualities, but that I would've found incredibly charming just the same.

But if you hadn't met me . . . I was going to write a list of everything you have because of me, beyond what you've sold, but it would be too long. You already know all the ways in which you've benefited from me, all the experiences you wouldn't have had otherwise. I mean, the first perfume you smelled in your life was a gift from me, for God's sake! I still remember how you bit through the plastic wrapper on the Dior at the airport . . .

If she were really so sorry, he tells her, she would've taken action to expiate her sins directly and immediately. *Acknowledging that the trust is broken beyond repair, that you are to blame, that you lack any credibility and all the rest is fine, but what is it worth?* A person really shows they're sorry for damage they've caused only when they're willing to pay for it. *Everything else is hot air coming out of their mouth.* Yes, Sonia agrees, but she already paid him the money, what else can she do?

Come, he says. *You can come see me and please me in every way I want, do whatever I tell you to do. One day. A single day of your life. A day devoted completely to me. It isn't much, considering I've been devoted to you for years.* What does he mean? she asks. *You can imagine. I want to do it to you knowing that you're wishing it was over. With absolute certainty that you're disgusted by me. I am completely serious. I'd love nothing more than to humiliate you, and afterward, when I finish, know that I have something of yours that you can't do anything to get back. Then you would know how you made me feel.*

Just who does he think she is? she says. He's basically asking her to be his prostitute. *There it is, more evidence of your contradictions,* Knut replies. *Not too long ago it was you who suggested that I use you sexually, that I do it to you with detachment and aggression. If I had judged your behavior as ugly back then, and said you were acting like a who . . . then you would've gotten angry.*

What's the problem with her doing what he asks for? It's the only possible way to atone: to do exactly what she wouldn't want to do. If a punishment consists of an action that doesn't perturb the recipient, it isn't a punishment. She has to feel the same way he felt to make it right. Actually, she needs to give herself over completely to the requests of the afflicted victim. *So your solution to pain is an eye for an eye?* she asks. No, Knut tells her. It wouldn't be possible to achieve that, the discomfort— the disgust, distress or whatever she wants to call it—that he's demanding of her is much less of a burden than the suffering he's endured. *You come one day, you do it, and you leave. Knowing you, you'll probably forget all about it in a couple of weeks.*

Confused, Sonia actually considers the option of going, but there's a boundary inside her she can't bring herself to cross. It isn't fear. It's not even a firm moral stance. It's a profound repulsion toward Knut, one she's felt since the very beginning. She realizes the core of her attraction has actually been this aversion: the chance to flirt with her antithesis.

Knut never wanted to sleep with her. All his fantasies were based on not touching and not naming. Now he demands sex as a form of degradation. A punishment. *The only possible way to atone*, he said. Sonia looks out the office window. Tiny cars neatly lined up in rows move forward slowly, curving around a large roundabout. They spin and spin like water around a drain.

Seen from a distance, things never change, she thinks.

No, she doesn't have to do anything she doesn't want to. *I'll never agree to something like that*, she tells him. She knows she's immune to any retaliation. She knows nothing will happen.

The scales tip in her favor.

What's the point of putting whipped cream on dog shit over and over again? she asks him. Why don't they stop it already? It's clear that she isn't worthy of him. She hasn't risen to the occasion, she hasn't appreciated what he's been offering her for so long. She doesn't deserve his attention or affection. So, why be stubborn and continue to write each other?

Precisely because of what's happened, Knut says, that's why they should continue. *You can't just cut me off. Just now is when you should stay, even if you don't like it. I'm the one who's been harmed, I'm the only one who gets to choose the retribution for the damage that I still have to deal with.*

I didn't mean it earlier when I said you should come and sleep with me so I could humiliate you. I was acting out of pain. But I am calm now. Calm and sad. Do you see how you put me in the position of being offended, hurt, but you don't help me get out of it? You don't give me what I need. And what I need right now is nothing other than for you to continue to write to me.

Sonia asks him why. What for? What does he get from it? Why does he cling to her? Hasn't she shown that she's incapable of appreciating him? Does he want to risk this happening again? *What I get out of it is between me and God. When you ask me my reasons, do you really want me to explain them to you? Are you going to take them into consideration? Or are you just going to say that well, you still feel the same way, and that you think we should stop anyway, after I've labored to ponder and expose all my reasons? Did you bother to think it through before asking? Don't you realize you make me vulnerable again by asking that? Have you thought that, when you ask something like that, there may actually be an answer?*

He asks her to try to see it from his point of view. To imagine herself doing for another man what he's done for her: treat her to gifts for years, write daily, share his thoughts on what he's reading, share his opinions, his experiences . . . How was he supposed to behave to prevent her from feeling smothered? Should he have been more patient? Just write to her and leave it at that? Not take it a millimeter further than a boundary they never set? Should he have disengaged, and waited until she decided to come back and reach out on her own, when he noticed the slightest distance? *I realize I made mistakes, I admit my flaws, that horrible combination of my paranoia and obsessiveness. But I can't think of a way I could've avoided them. Could you please tell me what I could've done? I just want to know. I'm solely interested in your psyche right now. Nothing else.*

She insists that it's absurd to continue. It only adds pain to the pain. They will always doubt each other's motives and the resentment will keep bubbling up. Knut replies that the pendulum will swing in both directions, that just as things got to this point they could have the opposite experience later. Everything was fine a little over a month ago. Why can't they make it work in the future? *I made you feel good once, didn't I? Don't you think it could happen again? What if I make an effort to improve? I will change anything you don't like about me,* he tells her. He asks her for another chance. They were born the same day on the same year. *Why so little faith? Don't I deserve anything anymore? If you reject me, you're also rejecting a part of your life . . . I mean reject in the sense of dismiss.* Why doesn't she try to give meaning to the relationship, at least in the end? Doesn't doing the opposite make her sad? *I'm sure people who get rid of their dogs think about it more and feel more remorse than you do right now.*

He still has some books for her. She didn't sell the books, did she? Did she sell any at all? She's kept them all since the beginning, right? That's at least a consolation. He doesn't think he'll ever be able to give her any perfume or lotion, and of course he won't give her any shoes or lingerie. But, if she doesn't mind, he'd like to send her these books. Sonia doesn't say anything. She knows there's no point in refusing. He'll send them anyway. The next day, Knut asks her to make a deposit for 18 euro for the shipping costs. *They're on the way,* he says.

The box was so heavy, he tells her, he almost couldn't carry it. He had to constantly shift the weight between his arms.

When he got to the post office and noticed it wouldn't be open
for another half hour, a realization hit him—it was brutal,
completely direct—he was going to miss that whole ritual. *You
already know: to miss a moment in the past is to miss who we were
in it.* In the afternoon, several hours later, he still got cramps
when flexing his arms. Overtaken by the sort of preemptive
nostalgia, he wondered if Sonia would experience nostalgia
in the future. *Will you miss this one day? Will you have another
relationship like ours, including the drawbacks? Do you think even
a rich man will give you the kinds of gifts I've given you? It's possible
that, if I become a millionaire, I'll give away much more than what
I've given you; but it would never, ever be in the same way. The
circumstances will simply be different and, not as good, I'm afraid.
Less worthy of being remembered.*

Knowing it was the last package he'd prepare for her in his
life—*it goes without saying that I will never do this for anyone
else*—he made sure to *procure* some titles he thinks are critical
for her to own. Her literary skill will thank him later, he assures
her. This gift has nothing to do with anything that happened
between them, it's solely about nurturing her talent, in which
he still firmly believes. He insists that she should write despite
everything. One day, she might even write about them, their
story. A story of the two of them as irrefutable evidence of the
power of fate. The world is unfair, he says, but life isn't. *I'm sure
that, in this perfect timepiece that is the universe, our differences—
or the fact that I wasn't ever able to see you wearing any of the
stockings I gave you—have their reasons for being. So, don't be
tormented by them.*

He wants to take the opportunity to make one last request.
It really is the last one, he tells her. Of the perfumes, which ones
did she sell? Which did she keep? For how much did she sell
them? Does she have the empty bottles? Are there any that still
have some perfume left? He'd like her to send the bottles as she
finishes the perfumes that she kept, if possible, and if she doesn't
mind. *No, of course I don't mind*, Sonia replies. *But I am slow*

to use them. I am sure you remember that was one of the reasons I gave you when I asked you not to give me any more. There's no rush, Knut says. She can send them whenever she finishes them, in her own time. Another way to keep the conversation going, Sonia thinks. And the questions, Knut adds. He asks her to please remember to answer his questions: which ones did she sell? Which ones did she keep? What were the dates, the prices?

They correspond some more. The last, agonizing death throes.

Sonia takes the books out of the box, she pages through them completely certain that they're the last ones because she's decided it. She thanks him, feeling sadness. *You're right,* she tells him. *I'll never have what I had with you with anyone else. Like you said, "once in a lifetime"...* She regrets that the final feeling is a bitter one. But she understands it's inevitable.

Don't worry, Knut says. *I still care about you. Tolstoy's advice for when you feel like you want to take revenge on someone is to think that they were once a child and that one day they will die.* For Knut that applies to Sonia more than anyone. The Sonia that betrayed him was also a child once, and one day, sooner or later, she will die too. *I will say this though: If I used to consider you a Salinger character, now I see you as Dostoievskian.*

He's the one who's felt pain. What Sonia has had to endure is feeling smothered, fed up. *Don't think I'm complaining, quite the opposite: I think your cross is much harder to bear.* Spiritual pain is as terrible as it is absurd, he tells her. He's had a couple of awful weeks, probably the worst in his life, but in a few months that pain will have dissipated, disappeared. *You, on the other hand, will carry the weariness I've caused you every time you're faced with a memory of me, every time a thought of me crosses your mind.* It's a fundamental difference.

I've given you everything, yes, but not what you wanted. Their bond, the things that brought them together, their shared affinities, those were all in his territory, not Sonia's. More than them meeting halfway, she would travel to where he was, to then return to her world, untouched.

But what you gave me . . . believe it or not, you are the only person—even if only from time to time—who's treated me like . . . like all of us want to be treated, like I wanted to be treated. You may ask yourself how my other relationships were. I ask myself the same thing about you.

It's over then? Definitely? Well, Knut replies, he'll always be willing to start over, however many years go by. No matter what she does to him, he'll always forgive her. *Not just because it's you, although yes, because of that too, but because deep down all that is meaningless. What's the worst thing you can imagine doing to me? That's nothing, absolutely nothing, that doesn't deserve to be forgiven.*

Sonia types slowly, carefully. The sun hasn't risen yet. The office is quiet; her coworkers, groggy, cold, trickle in silently. She looks up from the computer without actually looking at anything. The cause of her anxiety is uncertain. Relief finally comes, coupled with longing, inseparable from it. She writes one last time. She can almost feel him on the other side, wherever he's connected, his expectant breath, his constant checking for new email on the screen. *You'll forget me very soon*, she tells him. *Take care of yourself. Really, be good to yourself.*

Knut's response arrives immediately. *Right now I don't feel like I can forget you, but forgetting happens on its own, just like the passing of time. It will be harder for you to forget me. You'll see later on.*

If death doesn't grant my wish of disappearing in the most impersonal way possible, I'd like my epitaph to read: "I just wanted to escape."

Nothing else.

14. EPILOGUE

SHE LOOKS AROUND discreetly as they come out of the bookstore. Night has fallen and she can't make out all the faces in the crowd walking the streets full of businesses, food stands, sidewalk vendors, promotional booths, banks, signs, trash cans, *people and more people.* Loudness. Lights, confusion, noise. She's of course traveled to Cárdenas many more times after that first time, but the one that comes to mind now is the night of the dinner, when she hadn't met Knut. The lighting is identical, the time of day is the same as now. She remembers her amazement as she walked in the direction of the restaurant, her fascination with the group, the tediousness with which—she was barely aware of it then—she observed the evening unfold.

Her editor looks at her intently while he speaks. He's checking for a reaction, maybe a signal about how she feels, but she examines the vendors apprehensively, asking herself where he might be, which one he is, if he isn't hiding in the store in front of them, if he isn't the one waiting by that light post, or that man over there, walking away hunched with his back toward them, he has thick thighs and he's wearing long pointed shoes. No, his outfit's too informal, that other man's too tall, that one over there is bald but it's been a while, who knows. He wasn't back in the bookstore, she looked thoroughly and didn't see him. He definitely wasn't there during the presentation, it would've been impossible not to see him, so few people attended. He's not there, he didn't come. He really didn't come after all.

These events tend to go like this, the editor tells her. *Sometimes we have to cancel because no one shows. You shouldn't worry, it's not because of you.*

Sonia shakes her head no. *I'm not worried*, she replies in a dry tone.

She keeps searching without knowing what she's looking for. Knut's image, as if an image of him existed in her. What did he look like? She spent a day with him. An entire day. They kissed, even. They kissed three times, for a long time. They hugged. Something must be left from those hours and yet . . . what did he look like? Would she recognize him if she saw him? Knut is an amalgam of words, packages, labels written in all caps, bras, high heels, pictures, mirrors, security cameras, undercover security guards, cosmetic-dermatology clinics, books, more books, messages, pressure, lies, dreams. Right now she sees people, faces, she's in an actual place and time. It's too concrete for her to be able to find him. Her editor's scratchy voice rescues her out of her withdrawn trance.

What do you feel like doing? We could get a drink with the guys at the bar further up the road.

By *the guys* he means two bookstore employees that stayed behind to close up. They sold three books. *That's acceptable*, the editor affirms.

Sonia shrugs her shoulders. *Alright, yeah*, she says. *Let's go.*

They spend a couple of hours there. They sit by the bar drinking beer and timidly share an appetizer. The leftovers get cold on the plate until a waiter takes it away without asking. The editor takes out his wallet when the check comes and waves a bill. *This is on the press*, he says. *I can't be more broke than I already am!* They all laugh. The conversation has revolved around money the entire time. Deficits. Rights ownership. Sales, grants, economic crisis.

Sonia's tired. She wants to leave.

The cold air hits them when they step outside. There

aren't many people left out on the street. The cobblestones shine, coated by rain. It drizzled while they were inside. The sound of an organ-grinder is audible from far away. That sad and somehow tired-sounding melody they always play, like an out-of-tune lament. The editor gets close to Sonia to say goodbye. He has some food stuck in his teeth, they're sharp and yellowish. They kiss each other twice on the cheek politely, without affection.

Do you want to take a cab to the hotel? He offers to walk her to the taxi stop. Cárdenas starts to get a bit dangerous at that time of night. *Too many immigrants,* he says. *I don't mean it in a racist way,* he rushes to clarify. *It's just that poverty makes streets unsafe . . .*

The cab cruises around the nearly empty city. Sonia looks out the window. She notices a young woman in a miniskirt and a short fur coat walk disoriented between some rows of parked cars. The cabdriver makes a comment that Sonia doesn't quite hear. Something about alcohol and youth. Sonia gets impatient. The cab driver turns onto another street on a red light. And she sees it. She recognizes the street, the building. The old red block, with its ledges and tiny black windows, like holes that lead nowhere. It's completely abandoned now. A chain-link construction fence blocks the exterior. Scaffolding. Structures covered in the night's fog, like a scene in a science-fiction movie.

Stop here, she says.

Here? The cabdriver looks at her from the rearview mirror. *We're still far from the hotel.*

That's okay. Stop here. I'll get off here.

Did I say something that upset you? The cabdriver's tone is defiant, more angry than incredulous.

Sonia clarifies that *Oh no, no.* She just wants to get off here, that's all. She rushes to pay. She closes the car door softly, without taking her eyes off the building. She hears the taxi drive away until the engine sound fades completely.

To miss a moment in the past is to miss who we were in it.

The street looks deserted. Sonia starts to walk. Knut lives there now, she can't remember his building number. She sees more tall blocks with apartments and offices. Light shines through some of the windows. Blinds close, people walk fast from one room to another. She hears the fleeting racket of tires rumbling in the nearby streets. And finally a bus stops about thirty feet in front of her. The doors open with a screech, she hears the sound of compressed air releasing, a man gets off. It could be him. Yes, from behind, it could be him. Sonia stops. Her voice freezes inside her throat. She watches him walk. He's carrying shopping bags, he's wearing a suit. It could be him. Sonia takes a few steps forward, she stops again. He keeps walking at the same pace. His figure shrinks as he moves away. He dissipates. Disappears.

SARA MESA (Madrid, 1976) has lived in Seville since childhood. She is an award-winning author of poetry, fiction, and short stories. In addition to *Cicatriz* [*Scar*], her fiction and short stories include *Mala letra* [*Bad handwriting*] and *Cuatro por cuatro* [*Four by Four*].

ADRIANA NODAL-TARAFA is a professional translator and a graduate of University of Houston-Victoria and Dalkey Archive Press's Applied Literary Translation program. She also holds a Bachelor of Arts in Anthropology from the University of Washington.

MICHAL AJVAZ, *The Golden Age.*
The Other City.
PIERRE ALBERT-BIROT, *Grabinoulor.*
YUZ ALESHKOVSKY, *Kangaroo.*
FELIPE ALFAU, *Chromos.*
Locos.
JOE AMATO, *Samuel Taylor's Last Night.*
IVAN ÂNGELO, *The Celebration.*
The Tower of Glass.
ANTÓNIO LOBO ANTUNES, *Knowledge of Hell.*
The Splendor of Portugal.
ALAIN ARIAS-MISSON, *Theatre of Incest.*
JOHN ASHBERY & JAMES SCHUYLER, *A Nest of Ninnies.*
ROBERT ASHLEY, *Perfect Lives.*
GABRIELA AVIGUR-ROTEM, *Heatwave and Crazy Birds.*
DJUNA BARNES, *Ladies Almanack.*
Ryder.
JOHN BARTH, *Letters.*
Sabbatical.
DONALD BARTHELME, *The King.*
Paradise.
SVETISLAV BASARA, *Chinese Letter.*
MIQUEL BAUÇÀ, *The Siege in the Room.*
RENÉ BELLETTO, *Dying.*
MAREK BIENCZYK, *Transparency.*
ANDREI BITOV, *Pushkin House.*
ANDREJ BLATNIK, *You Do Understand.*
Law of Desire.
LOUIS PAUL BOON, *Chapel Road.*
My Little War.
Summer in Termuren.
ROGER BOYLAN, *Killoyle.*
IGNÁCIO DE LOYOLA BRANDÃO, *Anonymous Celebrity.*
Zero.
BONNIE BREMSER, *Troia: Mexican Memoirs.*
CHRISTINE BROOKE-ROSE, *Amalgamemnon.*
BRIGID BROPHY, *In Transit.*
The Prancing Novelist.

GERALD L. BRUNS, *Modern Poetry and the Idea of Language.*
GABRIELLE BURTON, *Heartbreak Hotel.*
MICHEL BUTOR, *Degrees.*
Mobile.
G. CABRERA INFANTE, *Infante's Inferno.*
Three Trapped Tigers.
JULIETA CAMPOS, *The Fear of Losing Eurydice.*
ANNE CARSON, *Eros the Bittersweet.*
ORLY CASTEL-BLOOM, *Dolly City.*
LOUIS-FERDINAND CÉLINE, *North.*
Conversations with Professor Y.
London Bridge.
MARIE CHAIX, *The Laurels of Lake Constance.*
HUGO CHARTERIS, *The Tide Is Right.*
ERIC CHEVILLARD, *Demolishing Nisard.*
The Author and Me.
MARC CHOLODENKO, *Mordechai Schamz.*
JOSHUA COHEN, *Witz.*
EMILY HOLMES COLEMAN, *The Shutter of Snow.*
ERIC CHEVILLARD, *The Author and Me.*
ROBERT COOVER, *A Night at the Movies.*
STANLEY CRAWFORD, *Log of the S.S. The Mrs Unguentine.*
Some Instructions to My Wife.
RENÉ CREVEL, *Putting My Foot in It.*
RALPH CUSACK, *Cadenza.*
NICHOLAS DELBANCO, *Sherbrookes.*
The Count of Concord.
NIGEL DENNIS, *Cards of Identity.*
PETER DIMOCK, *A Short Rhetoric for Leaving the Family.*
ARIEL DORFMAN, *Konfidenz.*
COLEMAN DOWELL, *Island People.*
Too Much Flesh and Jabez.
ARKADII DRAGOMOSHCHENKO, *Dust.*
RIKKI DUCORNET, *Phosphor in Dreamland.*
The Complete Butcher's Tales.

RIKKI DUCORNET (cont.), *The Jade Cabinet*.
The Fountains of Neptune.

WILLIAM EASTLAKE, *The Bamboo Bed*.
Castle Keep.
Lyric of the Circle Heart.

JEAN ECHENOZ, *Chopin's Move*.

STANLEY ELKIN, *A Bad Man*.
Criers and Kibitzers, Kibitzers and Criers.
The Dick Gibson Show.
The Franchiser.
The Living End.
Mrs. Ted Bliss.

FRANÇOIS EMMANUEL, *Invitation to a Voyage*.

PAUL EMOND, *The Dance of a Sham*.

SALVADOR ESPRIU, *Ariadne in the Grotesque Labyrinth*.

LESLIE A. FIEDLER, *Love and Death in the American Novel*.

JUAN FILLOY, *Op Oloop*.

ANDY FITCH, *Pop Poetics*.

GUSTAVE FLAUBERT, *Bouvard and Pécuchet*.

KASS FLEISHER, *Talking out of School*.

JON FOSSE, *Aliss at the Fire*.
Melancholy.

FORD MADOX FORD, *The March of Literature*.

MAX FRISCH, *I'm Not Stiller*.
Man in the Holocene.

CARLOS FUENTES, *Christopher Unborn*.
Distant Relations.
Terra Nostra.
Where the Air Is Clear.

TAKEHIKO FUKUNAGA, *Flowers of Grass*.

WILLIAM GADDIS, JR., *The Recognitions*.

JANICE GALLOWAY, *Foreign Parts*.
The Trick Is to Keep Breathing.

WILLIAM H. GASS, *Life Sentences*.
The Tunnel.
The World Within the Word.
Willie Masters' Lonesome Wife.

GÉRARD GAVARRY, *Hoppla! 1 2 3*.

ETIENNE GILSON, *The Arts of the Beautiful*.
Forms and Substances in the Arts.

C. S. GISCOMBE, *Giscome Road*.
Here.

DOUGLAS GLOVER, *Bad News of the Heart*.

WITOLD GOMBROWICZ, *A Kind of Testament*.

PAULO EMÍLIO SALES GOMES, *P's Three Women*.

GEORGI GOSPODINOV, *Natural Novel*.

JUAN GOYTISOLO, *Count Julian*.
Juan the Landless.
Makbara.
Marks of Identity.

HENRY GREEN, *Blindness*.
Concluding.
Doting.
Nothing.

JACK GREEN, *Fire the Bastards!*

JIŘÍ GRUŠA, *The Questionnaire*.

MELA HARTWIG, *Am I a Redundant Human Being?*

JOHN HAWKES, *The Passion Artist*.
Whistlejacket.

ELIZABETH HEIGHWAY, ED., *Contemporary Georgian Fiction*.

AIDAN HIGGINS, *Balcony of Europe*.
Blind Man's Bluff.
Bornholm Night-Ferry.
Langrishe, Go Down.
Scenes from a Receding Past.

KEIZO HINO, *Isle of Dreams*.

KAZUSHI HOSAKA, *Plainsong*.

ALDOUS HUXLEY, *Antic Hay*.
Point Counter Point.
Those Barren Leaves.
Time Must Have a Stop.

NAOYUKI II, *The Shadow of a Blue Cat*.

DRAGO JANČAR, *The Tree with No Name*.

MIKHEIL JAVAKHISHVILI, *Kvachi*.

GERT JONKE, *The Distant Sound*.
Homage to Czerny.
The System of Vienna.

JACQUES JOUET, *Mountain R.*
Savage.
Upstaged.
MIEKO KANAI, *The Word Book.*
YORAM KANIUK, *Life on Sandpaper.*
ZURAB KARUMIDZE, *Dagny.*
JOHN KELLY, *From Out of the City.*
HUGH KENNER, *Flaubert, Joyce and Beckett: The Stoic Comedians.*
Joyce's Voices.
DANILO KIŠ, *The Attic.*
The Lute and the Scars.
Psalm 44.
A Tomb for Boris Davidovich.
ANITA KONKKA, *A Fool's Paradise.*
GEORGE KONRÁD, *The City Builder.*
TADEUSZ KONWICKI, *A Minor Apocalypse.*
The Polish Complex.
ANNA KORDZAIA-SAMADASHVILI, *Me, Margarita.*
MENIS KOUMANDAREAS, *Koula.*
ELAINE KRAF, *The Princess of 72nd Street.*
JIM KRUSOE, *Iceland.*
AYSE KULIN, *Farewell: A Mansion in Occupied Istanbul.*
EMILIO LASCANO TEGUI, *On Elegance While Sleeping.*
ERIC LAURRENT, *Do Not Touch.*
VIOLETTE LEDUC, *La Bâtarde.*
EDOUARD LEVÉ, *Autoportrait.*
Newspaper.
Suicide.
Works.
MARIO LEVI, *Istanbul Was a Fairy Tale.*
DEBORAH LEVY, *Billy and Girl.*
JOSÉ LEZAMA LIMA, *Paradiso.*
ROSA LIKSOM, *Dark Paradise.*
OSMAN LINS, *Avalovara.*
The Queen of the Prisons of Greece.
FLORIAN LIPUŠ, *The Errors of Young Tjaž.*
GORDON LISH, *Peru.*
ALF MACLOCHLAINN, *Out of Focus.*
Past Habitual.

The Corpus in the Library.
RON LOEWINSOHN, *Magnetic Field(s).*
YURI LOTMAN, *Non-Memoirs.*
D. KEITH MANO, *Take Five.*
MINA LOY, *Stories and Essays of Mina Loy.*
MICHELINE AHARONIAN MARCOM, *A Brief History of Yes.*
The Mirror in the Well.
BEN MARCUS, *The Age of Wire and String.*
WALLACE MARKFIELD, *Teitlebaum's Window.*
DAVID MARKSON, *Reader's Block.*
Wittgenstein's Mistress.
CAROLE MASO, *AVA.*
HISAKI MATSUURA, *Triangle.*
LADISLAV MATEJKA & KRYSTYNA POMORSKA, EDS., *Readings in Russian Poetics: Formalist & Structuralist Views.*
HARRY MATHEWS, *Cigarettes.*
The Conversions.
The Human Country.
The Journalist.
My Life in CIA.
Singular Pleasures.
The Sinking of the Odradek.
Stadium.
Tlooth.
HISAKI MATSUURA, *Triangle.*
DONAL MCLAUGHLIN, *beheading the virgin mary, and other stories.*
JOSEPH MCELROY, *Night Soul and Other Stories.*
ABDELWAHAB MEDDEB, *Talismano.*
GERHARD MEIER, *Isle of the Dead.*
HERMAN MELVILLE, *The Confidence-Man.*
AMANDA MICHALOPOULOU, *I'd Like.*
STEVEN MILLHAUSER, *The Barnum Museum.*
In the Penny Arcade.
RALPH J. MILLS, JR., *Essays on Poetry.*
MOMUS, *The Book of Jokes.*
CHRISTINE MONTALBETTI, *The Origin of Man.*
Western.

NICHOLAS MOSLEY, *Accident.*
Assassins.
Catastrophe Practice.
A Garden of Trees.
Hopeful Monsters.
Imago Bird.
Inventing God.
Look at the Dark.
Metamorphosis.
Natalie Natalia.
Serpent.
WARREN MOTTE, *Fables of the Novel:*
French Fiction since 1990.
Fiction Now: The French Novel in the
21st Century.
Mirror Gazing.
Oulipo: A Primer of Potential Literature.
GERALD MURNANE, *Barley Patch.*
Inland.
YVES NAVARRE, *Our Share of Time.*
Sweet Tooth.
DOROTHY NELSON, *In Night's City.*
Tar and Feathers.
ESHKOL NEVO, *Homesick.*
WILFRIDO D. NOLLEDO, *But for*
the Lovers.
BORIS A. NOVAK, *The Master of*
Insomnia.
FLANN O'BRIEN, *At Swim-Two-Birds.*
The Best of Myles.
The Dalkey Archive.
The Hard Life.
The Poor Mouth.
The Third Policeman.
CLAUDE OLLIER, *The Mise-en-Scène.*
Wert and the Life Without End.
PATRIK OUŘEDNÍK, *Europeana.*
The Opportune Moment, 1855.
BORIS PAHOR, *Necropolis.*
FERNANDO DEL PASO, *News from*
the Empire.
Palinuro of Mexico.
ROBERT PINGET, *The Inquisitory.*
Mahu or The Material.
Trio.
MANUEL PUIG, *Betrayed by Rita*
Hayworth.

The Buenos Aires Affair.
Heartbreak Tango.
RAYMOND QUENEAU, *The Last Days.*
Odile.
Pierrot Mon Ami.
Saint Glinglin.
ANN QUIN, *Berg.*
Passages.
Three.
Tripticks.
ISHMAEL REED, *The Free-Lance*
Pallbearers.
The Last Days of Louisiana Red.
Ishmael Reed: The Plays.
Juice!
The Terrible Threes.
The Terrible Twos.
Yellow Back Radio Broke-Down.
JASIA REICHARDT, *15 Journeys Warsaw*
to London.
JOÃO UBALDO RIBEIRO, *House of the*
Fortunate Buddhas.
JEAN RICARDOU, *Place Names.*
RAINER MARIA RILKE,
The Notebooks of Malte Laurids Brigge.
JULIÁN RÍOS, *The House of Ulysses.*
Larva: A Midsummer Night's Babel.
Poundemonium.
ALAIN ROBBE-GRILLET, *Project for a*
Revolution in New York.
A Sentimental Novel.
AUGUSTO ROA BASTOS, *I the Supreme.*
DANIËL ROBBERECHTS, *Arriving in*
Avignon.
JEAN ROLIN, *The Explosion of the*
Radiator Hose.
OLIVIER ROLIN, *Hotel Crystal.*
ALIX CLEO ROUBAUD, *Alix's Journal.*
JACQUES ROUBAUD, *The Form of*
a City Changes Faster, Alas, Than the
Human Heart.
The Great Fire of London.
Hortense in Exile.
Hortense Is Abducted.
Mathematics: The Plurality of Worlds of
Lewis.
Some Thing Black.

RAYMOND ROUSSEL, *Impressions of Africa.*

VEDRANA RUDAN, *Night.*

PABLO M. RUIZ, *Four Cold Chapters on the Possibility of Literature.*

GERMAN SADULAEV, *The Maya Pill.*

TOMAŽ ŠALAMUN, *Soy Realidad.*

LYDIE SALVAYRE, *The Company of Ghosts.*
The Lecture.
The Power of Flies.

LUIS RAFAEL SÁNCHEZ, *Macho Camacho's Beat.*

SEVERO SARDUY, *Cobra & Maitreya.*

NATHALIE SARRAUTE, *Do You Hear Them?*
Martereau.
The Planetarium.

STIG SÆTERBAKKEN, *Siamese.*
Self-Control.
Through the Night.

ARNO SCHMIDT, *Collected Novellas.*
Collected Stories.
Nobodaddy's Children.
Two Novels.

ASAF SCHURR, *Motti.*

GAIL SCOTT, *My Paris.*

DAMION SEARLS, *What We Were Doing and Where We Were Going.*

JUNE AKERS SEESE, *Is This What Other Women Feel Too?*

BERNARD SHARE, *Inish.*
Transit.

VIKTOR SHKLOVSKY, *Bowstring.*
Literature and Cinematography.
Theory of Prose.
Third Factory.
Zoo, or Letters Not about Love.

PIERRE SINIAC, *The Collaborators.*

KJERSTI A. SKOMSVOLD, *The Faster I Walk, the Smaller I Am.*

JOSEF ŠKVORECKÝ, *The Engineer of Human Souls.*

GILBERT SORRENTINO, *Aberration of Starlight.*
Blue Pastoral.
Crystal Vision.

Imaginative Qualities of Actual Things.
Mulligan Stew. Red the Fiend.
Steelwork.
Under the Shadow.

MARKO SOSIČ, *Ballerina, Ballerina.*

ANDRZEJ STASIUK, *Dukla.*
Fado.

GERTRUDE STEIN, *The Making of Americans.*
A Novel of Thank You.

LARS SVENDSEN, *A Philosophy of Evil.*

PIOTR SZEWC, *Annihilation.*

GONÇALO M. TAVARES, *A Man: Klaus Klump.*
Jerusalem.
Learning to Pray in the Age of Technique.

LUCIAN DAN TEODOROVICI, *Our Circus Presents...*

NIKANOR TERATOLOGEN, *Assisted Living.*

STEFAN THEMERSON, *Hobson's Island.*
The Mystery of the Sardine.
Tom Harris.

TAEKO TOMIOKA, *Building Waves.*

JOHN TOOMEY, *Sleepwalker.*

DUMITRU TSEPENEAG, *Hotel Europa.*
The Necessary Marriage.
Pigeon Post.
Vain Art of the Fugue.

ESTHER TUSQUETS, *Stranded.*

DUBRAVKA UGRESIC, *Lend Me Your Character.*
Thank You for Not Reading.

TOR ULVEN, *Replacement.*

MATI UNT, *Brecht at Night.*
Diary of a Blood Donor.
Things in the Night.

ÁLVARO URIBE & OLIVIA SEARS, EDS., *Best of Contemporary Mexican Fiction.*

ELOY URROZ, *Friction.*
The Obstacles.

LUISA VALENZUELA, *Dark Desires and the Others.*
He Who Searches.

PAUL VERHAEGHEN, *Omega Minor.*

BORIS VIAN, *Heartsnatcher.*

LLORENÇ VILLALONGA, *The Dolls'
Room.*

TOOMAS VINT, *An Unending Landscape.*

ORNELA VORPSI, *The Country Where No
One Ever Dies.*

AUSTRYN WAINHOUSE, *Hedyphagetica.*

CURTIS WHITE, *America's Magic
Mountain.*
The Idea of Home.
Memories of My Father Watching TV.
Requiem.

DIANE WILLIAMS,
Excitability: Selected Stories.
Romancer Erector.

DOUGLAS WOOLF, *Wall to Wall.*
Ya! & John-Juan.

JAY WRIGHT, *Polynomials and Pollen.*
The Presentable Art of Reading Absence.

PHILIP WYLIE, *Generation of Vipers.*

MARGUERITE YOUNG, *Angel in the
Forest.*
Miss MacIntosh, My Darling.

REYOUNG, *Unbabbling.*

VLADO ŽABOT, *The Succubus.*

ZORAN ŽIVKOVIĆ , *Hidden Camera.*

LOUIS ZUKOFSKY, *Collected Fiction.*

VITOMIL ZUPAN, *Minuet for Guitar.*

SCOTT ZWIREN, *God Head.*

AND MORE . . .